Also by Karen Musser Nortman

The Frannie Shoemaker Campground Mysteries
We are NOT Buying a Camper! (prequel)
Bats and Bones
The Blue Coyote
The Lady of the Lake
To Cache a Killer
A Campy Christmas
The Space Invader

The Time Travel Trailer Series
The Time Travel Trailer
Trailer on the Fly

peete and repeat

A Frannie Shoemaker Campground Mystery

by Karen Musser Nortman

Cover Artwork by Gretchen Musser
Cover Design by Libby Shannon

Dedicated to my children and grandchildren
Andy and Stacy
Pat and Jill
Kate and Ron
Brooke, Ty, Tuan, Jessi, Steven, Jack, Sophie and
Elliot

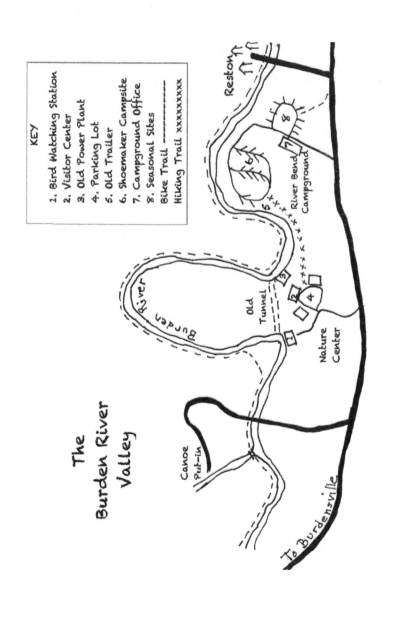

The
Burden River
Valley

KEY

1. Bird Watching Station
2. Visitor Center
3. Old Power Plant
4. Parking Lot
5. Old Trailer
6. Shoemaker Campsite
7. Campground Office
8. Seasonal Sites
Bike Trail ————
Hiking Trail xxxxxxxx

Reston

River Bend
Campground

Burden River

Old
Tunnel

Nature
Center

Canoe
Put-in

To Burdensville

TABLE OF CONTENTS

PROLOGUE

FOUR YEARS EARLIER

VIRGINIA WAS ABOUT to close the laptop, but decided to check her sister's account, automatically entering the password. The screen showed ten or twelve unopened emails—half a dozen ads for online clothing and photo outlets, three forwards of feel-good slogans and pictures from an annoying cousin, two notices from volunteer groups about upcoming events, and one from an unfamiliar personal email address that had just arrived. She clicked on it and glanced over it, then reread it carefully, leaning toward the screen.

"Dear Val," it said. "I can't tell you how much I have missed you since arriving home. What an amazing time we had. My sister has tried to talk me into a cruise for years and I always thought it sounded stupid. How wrong I was! I just got back from the business trip to Spain that I told you about and I have to see you again. I have a short layover in Minneapolis on Friday—can I come by right after lunch? I love you—Richard."

She closed the email, marked it as unread, and sat back in her chair. Her face flushed and her stomach clenched. Reconsidering, she opened the email again and hit *Reply*.

1

"Dear Richard, I would like to see you again. Can I just meet you at the airport? Love, Val." She hit *Send*. She examined the email address: ellis-reynolds@hotmail.com. So was his name Richard Ellis-Reynolds?

While she waited, her anger built. No wonder Valerie was so upbeat when she returned home from the cruise. Oh, she feigned great sympathy with Virginia for being sick and missing out on the trip they had planned together, but it never seemed sincere. Now she knew why.

"C'mon," she said through her teeth. "Answer."

The notifier pinged.

"Dear Val, That would be great. I will be coming in at gate C15 at 12:10. See you then! Love, Richard."

She hit *Reply* again. "Dear Richard, I will be there. I have something important to tell you. If there is any change in plans, text me at 407-555-2187. Our email is very sporadic. Love, Val." She stopped, deleted 'our,' typed 'my' and hit *Send*. Then she deleted the two emails from him, went into the 'sent' file and deleted hers.

Next she did a search on Richard Ellis-Reynolds. She found one who was a broker for a large well-known securities firm in Chicago. Possible. The cruise that she and Valerie had signed up for was handled by a midwestern travel agency. Ellis-Reynolds could be a company name, but not likely with a hotmail address.

Virginia sighed. Valerie was so naive when it came to men. She supposed she would have to rescue her sister again and then pick up the pieces.

She was back at the laptop that afternoon, working on some digitized photos for a local magazine when she heard the connecting door to the garage open.

"Ginny? Are you here?"

She gritted her teeth. Valerie called her that just to annoy her, but Virginia wasn't going to let her sister get a rise out of her today, so she saved her work and closed the laptop.

"I was in the office," she called out as she headed to the kitchen. Valerie unloaded her purse and a sack of groceries on the counter. She turned to face Virginia, her face flushed from the warm day and framed with downy blonde curls. A mirror image. Virginia always reveled in the knowledge that Valerie's clear blue eyes behind stylish glasses, somewhat round face, and full mouth were what people also saw when they looked at her. Of course, the drawback to being an identical twin was being reminded of one's own aging as the lines around the mouth and eyes on her sister increased with middle age.

"Any calls?" Valerie asked as she started to stash items in the refrigerator. After her discoveries earlier, Virginia could now identify a hopeful note in Valerie's voice.

"No, why? Were you expecting some?"

"No, no," Valerie turned, folding the reusable shopping bag and storing it in a rack beside the refrigerator. "Not particularly. Everyone's been asking about you at work. I told them I thought you are planning to come back Monday. Is that still true?"

3

"Oh, definitely. I'm actually taking this week as vacation. I've been working on that *Solomon's Seal* order the last couple of days."

They continued chatting about work projects as they collaborated on a pasta dish and salad for supper. Virginia watched her sister, noting a distracted manner that she hadn't been aware of before. It was time to nip this in the bud before Valerie became any more involved. She would be sad for a while but she would get over it. She always had before.

ON FRIDAY, AFTER VALERIE had left for work, Virginia showered, dressed and took extra care with her hair and makeup. She would have to put on a good act, but she had been doing that for years. People gravitated to Valerie because Virginia could be impatient, a little controlling, and, well, maybe a touch arrogant. So she often put on a more Valerie-like demeanor to keep things even. If people liked Valerie too much, they would take advantage of her. It was for Valerie's own good.

By 11:45, she was at Gate C15, seated where she had a good view of arrivals but wouldn't be immediately spotted. In her online search, she had found a picture of Richard Ellis-Reynolds so that she knew who to watch for. The flight was a little early and passengers started coming through the door about noon. Richard Ellis-Reynolds was the sixth person to emerge. She rose, and walked slowly toward the passengers, giving herself time to size him up before he saw her.

He was medium height, had dark short hair with a pronounced widow's peak, impressive eyebrows and a small cleft in his chin. He was neither brutally handsome nor bad to look at. He wore a tan suit, light blue shirt, and striped tie. As he twisted to sling the strap of a laptop case over his shoulder, he glanced her way, saw her and broke into a broad smile.

"Val!" He hurried over and engulfed her in an awkward hug. She let loose a peal of nervous laughter, one of the things she liked least about herself. He held her back and stared at her.

"I have missed that laugh—and everything about you!"

"It's only been a week and a half, Richard."

"I know, I know, way too long!" He took her elbow and steered her toward the bar. "Shall we get a drink? Have you had lunch? Do you have time?"

She laughed again, less cautious now that she knew he liked it. "Richard, one question at a time. A drink would be fine, I've had lunch, but yes, I have time."

They found a secluded booth and he motioned the waiter over, ordering himself a Manhattan and her a glass of Valerie's favorite white wine.

He grinned at her, beside himself at seeing her again. "Something has to change. I can't stand this. I thought seeing you every couple of weeks would be sufficient, but—," he shook his head, serious now. "Val, darling, I want to ask you—."

She put up her hand to shush him. "Richard," she said, and on cue a tear started down her cheek. "I told you I had something to tell you, and it won't be pleasant for either of us."

The waiter brought the drinks, and Richard handed him a folded bill, waving him away without taking his eyes off her. "What are you saying...?"

She took a sip of her wine and held her other hand up again. "I can't do this, Richard. I can't tell you why right now, but please know that I do love you. I just can't—I *cannot* continue our relationship."

He leaned forward, anger and shock on his face. "What are you talking about?" His voice was raised, and as soon as he said it, he looked around the bar to see if he was attracting too much attention. A few faces turned their way. This was why she wanted to meet him at the airport. Any scene would be easier to control.

She let the tears flow freely now, daintily wiping them with a tissue from her purse. "Please, don't make this harder..."

"Harder?" he whispered hoarsely. "How can it be any harder? I thought we really had something. Less than two weeks ago, you said you would love me forever. What has changed? Family problems?—but you said you had no family..."

Virginia seethed at that last statement but she controlled her anger. "Richard," she said faintly, "please try to understand...," she stopped and waved away his objections, "okay, if not understand, *accept* what I am saying. I have no choice, and it is unfair to you to drag this out. Forget about me and don't try to contact me any more. If you hear from me, it is only a momentary weakness; don't respond." She let her voice become stronger, firmer, but no louder. "I mean it when I say that I cannot continue seeing you—and that's all I can say. I wish you the best and know you will find someone else who is worthy of you." She slid to the edge of the booth, quickly getting up, and turning away from him. As she walked out of the bar, she glanced in the mirror above the bar to gauge his reaction. He appeared devastated. Not until she had walked out of the building did she allow herself a small smile. Val, darling, indeed.

CHAPTER ONE
FRIDAY AFTERNOON

THEY HAD STARTED out from southeastern Iowa early in the morning in a caravan of four camping units. The clouds formed a hammock that hung from the sky and dripped intermittently. About ten miles out of town, after a frantic cell phone call, the entire group pulled off on the shoulder. Jane Ann and Mickey Ferraro turned their red and white motorhome, the "Red Rocket," around and went back home to turn off the oven and get the cake Mickey had baked that morning.

Waiting, Frannie and Larry Shoemaker relaxed in their pickup cab. Their thirty-foot Fleetwood Terry travel trailer blocked the rear view of the rest of the group. But in the extended side mirrors, Frannie could see Ben Terell's yellow pickup and his and Nancy's hybrid trailer —a small trailer with drop-down ends containing the beds. Behind them in another pickup, Rob and Donna Nowak pulled a tan Winnebago trailer festooned with swirling brown graphics. Frannie thought all they needed was a truck pulling a cage with a lion in it. Or maybe even a small elephant.

The group often camped together and once a year took a long weekend in southeastern Minnesota, camping along the Burden River and enjoying the bike trail. The Shoemakers and the Ferraros were retired; the others hoped to follow suit in the next few years. The Ferraros returned, heading on down the road, and the others pulled out behind them.

After a brief early lunch stop, the Shoemakers were again in the lead. Larry tuned the radio to an oldies station and Frannie let her mind wander. She found camping with their friends a wonderful escape. Not that she faced any great traumas at home these days; just that there was always some little job that needed doing, and Larry did not know how to procrastinate. "Maybe we should clean the basement today?" or "Since it's a nice day, we oughta get those porch windows washed." Always something. Frannie wasn't lazy. She had been a teacher for thirty-five years, raised kids, done her share of volunteering. But now, she was more than willing to forego the basement to finish the book she was reading. Or do almost anything else.

When they camped, their routines were so well-established; the few chores were shared by everyone and required little effort. The only work was fixing meals, and they had turned that into entertainment. The Ferraros were their most frequent companions; Jane Ann was Larry's sister, younger by two years, and had been one of Frannie's best friends since she and Larry were married. Mickey and Larry were close too, although no one would know it to listen to them. Ben resembled a cartoon leprechaun and was a successful physical therapist.

Nancy, a community organizer, also used her skills to try and keep the group on track.

Rob and Donna had a small accounting firm. Rob could always be counted on for entertainment: funny stories, outrageous lights on his camper, and practical jokes. And Donna—well, Donna was Donna. But Frannie anticipated the conversations around the fire, the food, and the biking.

A muffled 'pop' interrupted her reverie, and the steering wheel jerked to the right in Larry's hands. He edged the pickup off the road and turned on his blinkers.

Frannie sat up and looked at him. "A tire?"

"I hope not," Larry answered as they both got out. The others had passed them and pulled over as well. The problem was obvious. One of the tandem tires on the passenger side of the trailer shredded into dozens of inch-wide strips sprouting from the rim like one of those giant homecoming mums. But not as pretty or festive.

Larry rubbed his short grey crewcut as the mist clouded his glasses and said, "Crap."

The others had also disembarked and walked toward them, huddled in slickers and windbreakers. When Rob, now at the front of the line, saw the tire, he said, "There's a town just a mile or so ahead."

"I don't know if I dare drive on it. I'd have to go so slow, I'd probably get rear ended."

But, in an unexpected stroke of luck, a patrol car drew up behind the trailer. After the deputy saw the evidence of their plight, he told Larry to continue into town on the shoulder and he would run interference. The others were given directions to a tire repair shop and told to go on ahead, which they did, relieved to get out of the rain, the tire-changing, and the decision-making responsibilities.

After what seemed like a long and harrowing trip into the small town, but in reality was fairly short and safe, they pulled in at a small old garage. Several scruffy-looking men sat just inside the open garage door, watching the rain drip and the world go by. Decades of dirt and grease gave the whole scene a monochromatic shade of gray. The smell of oil and stale ashtrays reached even the driveway outside.

The deputy waved and continued down the road, and Larry explained the situation to the owner. Between them, they located the spare, and the owner and one of his cronies efficiently went about replacing the shredded tire. The charge was quite minor, but came with adamant advice about replacing the trailer tires every five years, since, even though they would have low miles, they would tend to dry out and rot from sun and sitting. The men in the garage called out other advice and exchanged jibes, laughing at the travelers' predicament. Before they left, the owner also gave Larry the names of a couple of tire dealers and suppliers on their way who could replace all of the tires with new. For more than a minor charge, of course.

Meanwhile, the Nowaks and the Terells had gone on ahead, while Mickey and Jane Ann elected to wait for Larry and Frannie in case of further mishap. But, until they reached the nearest tire dealer, Frannie kept an eye glued to the side mirror, should the spare decide to explode or fly off into the cornfields. She was much relieved when the first dealer they stopped at could replace all four tires with new ones even though it delayed them another hour and a half, and would take a chunk out of their retirement budget.

The terrain of Northeast Iowa always fascinated her. The rolling fields they had passed farther south morphed into steeper and steeper hills. The highway cut through many of the taller bluffs, exposing walls of sandstone and dolostone. Gone were the straight highways of the southern and central parts of the state, replaced by twisting asphalt ribbons. The rain lifted before they reached Minnesota and, as they dropped down into the Burden River Valley, most of the clouds had even dissipated.

The sites at the River Bend campground nestled around several loops of the road in a low flat area, surrounded by the hills and bluffs of southeastern Minnesota. The main attraction of the area, a beautiful sixty-mile bike trail connecting several small towns, ran along the other side of the Burden River. The blue of the sky and green of the grass and trees were so intense, it almost hurt the eyes.

Looking around as Larry checked in at the campground office, Frannie thought it should seem like the start of a perfect weekend. However, getting here this time wasn't 'half the fun,' as one of their group said all too frequently.

By the time the Shoemakers and Ferraros had parked and set up their campers in adjoining sites, it was early afternoon. Ben and Nancy were in the site on the other side of Frannie and Larry; Rob and Donna were right across the road. Rob and Ben had already dragged two picnic tables together and Donna and Nancy had covered them with bright vinyl tablecloths. The Terells' terrier/boxer, Chloe and Nowak's schnauzer, Buster were tethered near the chairs in the shade. Frannie added their old yellow Lab, Cuba, to the menagerie.

Donna and Rob walked over from their site. "We should have taken those sites up there." She pointed up the slope to the next row, slightly more shaded. Donna was never happy with any site they had.

"These are easier to get into," Frannie couldn't resist pointing out.

"I suppose." Donna grudgingly agreed. "Hey, did you notice that little trailer next to us? Isn't it adorable?"

They looked across the road where she pointed at a small white squarish trailer with gray trim, partially hidden by Nowak's unit.

"What is it?" Ben asked. "It doesn't look familiar at all."

"It says 'Kraus' or 'Knaus' or something on it," Donna said.

"German, maybe? I'll have to check the 'net," Rob said. They stared a moment and then returned to their plans.

"I've done an excellent job of arranging the weather for this weekend," Mickey said. "70s and no more rain in sight."

"Can we get that in writing?" Rob laughed at him. "Speaking of perfect weather, are we riding this afternoon?"

"We certainly have time," Larry said. "Maybe just the stretch from Reston to Burdensville?"

"And do a little shopping at Burdensville?" Donna asked.

"And have a little pie at the Reston Pie Shoppe when we get back," Frannie added.

"I suspected there would be pie involved when I suggested it," Rob said. And to his wife, "If you're shopping, do I need to drive the truck over?"

Donna grinned. "No, I have a basket. Jewelry doesn't take much space."

Rob rubbed his head in mock despair and they unloaded their bikes from the backs of trailers and pickup beds.

THE CAMPGROUND WAS across the river from the trail; to get to the trail they first followed a path along the eastern end of the campground. The campsites on this end were seasonal sites, occupied by large trailers and fifth wheels, and rented for the summer. Some even had small wooden decks with pots of geraniums and perennial plantings around the edges. Frannie noticed that their favorite, a trailer made to look like a log cabin, sat in the same site again this year.

The group pedaled on a gravel trail to the highway, rode along the shoulder for a quarter of a mile to the bridge, and then across the bridge to Reston and the paved bike trail. At the trailhead, they pulled out water bottles for a little refreshment and then headed west toward Burdensville, five miles away.

The trail was shaded, but they caught glimpses between the trees of the sun sparkling off the river. Rob pointed out their campground across the river as they passed. Quaint bridges over picturesque ravines and streams tumbling to join the river broke up the ride. At the end of one such bridge, a small clearing held a bench and a rustic information kiosk. Mickey and Donna collapsed on the bench, while Frannie and Jane Ann examined the postings in the kiosk. One flyer printed on green paper sported a sketch of a building and information about the 'Old Power Plant.'

Frannie peered at the sketch, and then turned around and looked across the river between an opening in the trees. She pointed and said to Jane Ann, "That's what that building is. I've noticed it every year but never knew what it was."

A large, gray, monolithic shell of a building clung to the steep cliff along the river. Discoloration streaked its face, almost like the tracks of tears. It appeared to be on the verge of being engulfed by the trees and other vegetation all around it, seeming to grow out of the cliff.

Nancy looked up from kneeling to retie one of her shoes. "What?"

"An old power plant over there," Frannie said. "There's a poster on the kiosk about it."

Nancy stood. "Oh, right. There's a great nature center on the hill above it—you can't see it from here, but Ben and I stopped there once when we were up here by ourselves. I think there's a hiking path from the campground to the center—maybe a mile and a half. We should put that on our schedule for the weekend." Nancy loved schedules.

Donna rose from the bench and hobbled over to join them. Jane Ann looked back at her. "What's the matter, Donna? Knee trouble?"

"No," Donna said a little sheepishly. "I just got these shoes, and I thought they were *so* cute, but they didn't have my size so they might be a little small." Donna, being the shortest, barged to the front of the group of women. "What are you looking at?"

"That building—it's an old power plant," Frannie said. It dominated the other side of the river.

"Oh, wow," Donna said, swinging her camera up and moving down the sloping bank as she said it. Her foot caught in a tree root and she started to pitch forward. She caught herself by grabbing a small tree trunk, but not before one of its branches slapped her on the face.

"Ow! Dammit!" she yelped. Nancy rushed to her aid, while Frannie and Jane Ann exchanged wry glances. These antics were to be expected with Donna. Jane Ann, a retired nurse, examined the scratch when Donna got back up to the sidewalk, and pronounced it survivable.

"It feels awfully close to my eye," Donna said, as she limped back to her bike.

They mounted their bikes again and, with some false starts and a little wobbling, continued on the path. Since their speed was moderate, to be generous, they were often passed and more frequently met by other cyclists and a few hikers.

As they neared Burdensville, the path crossed another wooden bridge over a deep ravine and wound up a gradual hill. Coming around a gentle curve, a pair of hikers approached them. It was like double vision. Two middle-aged women in matching cowboy hats, printed t-shirts, and khaki shorts moved along briskly. Their faces and blonde hair were identical, their fanny packs slung in the same manner, their strides in unison.

Frannie's group met and glided by the two hikers, but they caught a glimpse of quick smiles and nods of greeting. Frannie looked at Donna, riding next to her, and saw the same look of astonishment that she felt on her own face.

"Wow," was all Donna could say, uncharacteristically brief. Further discussion faded as they focused on climbing the gentle grade of the hill. Before long they rode into the outskirts of town and concentrated on watching for stop signs at street crossings and signs pointing to the business district.

Larry, in the lead, stopped when they reached the center of town. After conferring with Rob, he led the group down the cross street to an area three blocks long of old rehabbed store fronts, theaters, bed and breakfasts, and restaurants. The sidewalks were raised and fronted with angled parking spaces alternating with bike racks. Larry and Rob chose a rack in front of a restaurant as a landing spot for the group.

They spent the next couple of hours roaming the shops and exploring a small museum. The smell of baking bread sucked them into a small bakery where Donna bought cinnamon rolls for the next day's breakfast and Mickey purchased two pounds of his favorite coffee.

"We'd better head back if we're going to have time to stop for pie," Rob said.

"You may have to take me to the emergency room," Donna said to him, suddenly remembering her injury.

"We'll see—it's hardly noticeable." Rob was used to appeasing his wife and knew that she was most concerned with how she looked. They returned to their bikes, stashed their purchases and were soon heading back east on the bike trail.

On the return, Frannie watched for the old power plant. Its solid, almost windowless face fascinated her but also gave her a sense of foreboding. When she spotted it, she asked Nancy, "Can you get down to that power plant from the nature center?"

"I think there's an old path, but they don't encourage it. We didn't try it when we were there."

As they neared Reston, they caught up to the twin hikers. Frannie wondered what life would be like, looking in a mirror constantly. But the appearance up ahead of the Pie Shoppe distracted her, as anything offering dessert was wont to do.

CHAPTER TWO
LATE FRIDAY AFTERNOON

The Reston Pie Shoppe was a white frame building standing alone on a side street off the tiny business district. Four large bike racks along the front and one side attested to the nature of the clientele. The group parked their bikes and tromped in through a side door. Jane Ann and Donna headed for the restroom. Everyone else stood at the counter staring up at the ten-foot long blackboard on the wall proclaiming the day's offerings.

Frannie scrunched up her face and agonized. She loved pie. Deciding what kind to have at anytime was one of life's most difficult inconsequential decisions; at places like this she verged on collapse.

"What are you having?" she said to Larry, next to her. Like it mattered. They didn't have the same favorites and in no way would his choice influence hers. It was a stalling tactic. She had to decide first what type she wanted this time: fruit, cream or chiffon. And then one crust or two? Once she narrowed her choices, she would consider which of those kinds she would be least likely to make herself, and it had to be one no one else was ordering.

He said, "Apple, I guess."

"Bor-ring," she said, although she did love a good apple pie. On the other side of Rob, Mickey ordered butterscotch, another of her favorites.

"I'll have the fresh blackberry," she blurted out to the forty-something woman behind the counter, and was immediately besieged by doubts. Maybe she should have ordered lemon meringue; she couldn't make meringue to save her soul and they were masters here. She was about to change her order when she noticed Larry watching her and laughing.

"What?!"

"You. You're thinking about changing your order, aren't you? We'll be here five days; you can come back every day."

"I can come back *two* or *three* times a day if I want. I don't need your permission," she retorted. The woman set a heavy white china plate in front of her, with a fragrant heap of purple berries and golden brown lattice crust.

"I'm sorry—it's just out of the oven and didn't come out of the pan very well. And I should mention that they *are* fresh blackberries but not local—a little early for that yet. I can get you something different if you'd like."

Frannie picked up the plate. "Absolutely not. This looks wonderful." She shot her husband a defiant look, grabbed a fork out of the container on the counter, and carried her pie to a table where Mickey and Ben were already seated. Donna and Jane Ann had returned from the restroom, Donna looking much relieved that the scratch was negligible, but still limping. The others soon joined them and dug in, trading bites and offering deep, introspective critiques such as "Wow!" and "Mmmm."

Frannie glanced up at the sound of the front door opening. The two women they had passed on the path entered and walked to the counter. Under their cowboy hats, their chin-length blonde hair fell in soft waves framing their round faces, reminding Frannie of the women in the old "Beautiful Hair-Breck" ads both in color and texture — pale and very fine. They moved as one, and both placed their right elbows on the counter, ordering "Cherry pie, please," in unison. The counter woman didn't know for sure how to react, and with obvious effort kept her expression very neutral, but pleasant.

The women carried their pie to an open table, slung their cameras on the right corner of their chair backs and seated themselves with identical movements. Uncanny.

Mickey poked Frannie in the thigh. "Close your mouth," he said with a grin, "your pie will fall out."

She did, and wiped the edges of her mouth with her napkin.

"Don't you think it's kind of odd? How do they even do that?" she whispered back at him.

"Habit, I guess. They must spend a lot of time together," he said quietly.

"Anyone up for going farther or are you all wimping out?" Ben asked the group.

"Wimping." "Wimping." "Ditto."

"I'd go a little farther, " Rob said. "What are we doing for supper?"

"Brats," Nancy said. "Simple, and we all brought sides ready to eat, so you guys have time to ride further if you want."

"What about you?" Rob said to his wife. "Do we need to go to the hospital?"

"No, I'll be fine," Donna said. She touched her cheek, grimaced, and put on her bravest look.

The front door opened again and a tall man decked in serious biking attire came in. Frannie was watching the twins' synchronized actions, when the man in biking gear, having purchased only a bottle of water, (who does that in a pie shop?) turned just as one of the women looked up from their conversation. Her mouth dropped open and an anguished expression crossed her face. Her sister followed her gaze, but frowned and set her mouth as if gritting her teeth. It was the first difference between the two that Frannie had observed. The man, in turn, eyed them both, confused. He seemed about to speak but thought better of it, turned, and hurried outside.

Through the front windows, Frannie could see him mount his bike and head off in the direction of Burdensville. She glanced back to the twins, oblivious to the conversation around her. The angry twin had recovered her equanimity and reached across the table to take her sister's hand, apparently asking what had upset the other. The second shook her head and pulled her hand back, turned her head and covered her mouth. She seemed to regain her composure and returned to her pie, as did her sister. They didn't speak until they finished, but occasionally each stole glances at the other.

Very strange, thought Frannie. Something about the man shattered their years of habit and ripped them apart, like Siamese twins being separated, in the blink of an eye. Frannie loved a good mystery but didn't see any way she would solve this one without being downright nosey. And while she wasn't averse to subtly poking around for information, she could hardly ask complete strangers outright to explain such an odd relationship.

"Hey, zombie," Larry broke into her trance, "Ready to go?"

She looked at her plate. Her pie was gone. How annoying—she had finished it without even enjoying it. She slid out of her chair and carried her plate to a bin of dirty dishes. They all trooped outside and readied their bikes.

While Frannie strapped on her helmet, the twins emerged from the cafe, both looking very strained. They headed down the bike path toward Newton, not talking. Rob and Ben took off in the same direction, while the rest turned toward the bridge.

Frannie pedaled along beside Jane Ann as they reached the gravel path on the other side of the river.

"Did you watch those twins?"

"You mean when that guy came in? Really odd, wasn't it? Looked like they knew each other but never spoke," Jane Ann said.

"Well, yeah—up until then they were like synchronized swimmers—every movement matched. Very weird."

They continued in silence, the uneven nature of the path requiring their full attention. Back at their campsite, they arranged their lounge chairs in the shade, and retrieved books and beverages from their campers.

Donna sat down and gingerly removed her tennis shoes and socks. Her toes and heels sported several angry red blisters and she studied them with dismay.

"I need my sandals," she said, looking at her camper on the other side of the gravel road. "Nancy, would you mind? They're right inside the door."

Nancy had just stretched out in a lounge chair with her book, but started to get up. Frannie, still moving her chair, said, "Stay there. I'll get them."

"Would you untie Buster, too, and bring him over?" Donna called after her. They all knew that Donna was the 'high maintenance' member of the group and that wasn't likely to change, so Frannie just nodded.

As she unhooked Buster's tether, she got a good look at the little trailer they had talked about earlier. It was boxier than American-made trailers and quite plain with a European-minimalist air about it. A small red pickup was parked near it but no sign of habitation. She led Buster back and, after she handed Donna the sandals, tethered him to a nearby tree.

"Could you get him some water, too?" Donna said, and as an afterthought, "Please?"

The next hour passed with some dozing, some reading, and very occasional subdued conversation.

Wheels crunched on gravel, and Rob and Ben rode back into the campsite. They stowed their bikes and helmets and joined the rest of the group.

"You ride all the way to Newton?" Mickey asked.

"Actually, we did," Ben said. "We can go pretty fast when you guys aren't holding us back."

"A little excitement on the trail, though," Rob said. "Remember those twins we saw?"

Frannie sat up, more alert, and Donna said, "What about 'em?"

"When we passed them coming back, they were in the midst of a shouting match," Rob said.

"Really?" Donna said. "What about? Did it have to do with that guy in the pie shop? What were they saying?"

"We didn't stop and ask if we could listen in on their conversation," Rob said.

"Oh, right," Donna sat back, disappointed.

"Rob wanted to," Ben smiled.

"So did you," Rob retorted.

"Well, we'll never know," Frannie said. "I think it's time to start some supper."

Larry got up and assembled his swing-away grill—an ingenious arrangement with a grill suspended from a crosspiece on a single pole pounded into the ground next to the fire ring. Mickey added wood to the fire while the rest of the group brought the prepared dishes, brats, buns and tableware out of their campers. Rob and Ben took over cooking the brats.

Several other units had pulled in and the campground gradually filled up. Children and dogs seemed to be everywhere, while their parents were occupied with getting food on the table, some simple, some elaborate.

The group passed the bright-colored bowls and plates of food, while hungrily eying each offering. Frannie savored the juicy brats, a high-fat indulgence that she rarely allowed herself, as well as the marinated fresh asparagus, a wonderful strawberry spinach salad, and German potato salad. Mickey complimented her potato salad and then took a big bite of his brat, nestled in a bun and covered with mustard.

"Ack!" he said, spitting it out into a napkin. "Nowak! You did that!"

Rob looked up, straight faced and innocent. "What?" Everyone else, looked at Mickey, puzzled.

"What was that about?" Jane Ann said.

Mickey opened the bun and held it out. "Plastic brat," he said. "I knew Rob was a bad cook, but didn't realize how bad."

The group erupted in laughter, and Larry leaned over and pounded Rob on the back. "Nice one, Rob!" Rob stood up and took a little bow.

They returned to their meal and were just finishing up when Donna, on the side of the picnic table facing the entrance road, dramatically whispered "Look!"

Frannie turned in her seat just long enough to glimpse the twins approaching their area. But they continued on past Nowak's trailer and disappeared into the little German unit.

"Verrry interesting!" Rob said in his best Dracula accent.

One of the twins came back out, minus the cowboy hat, and headed up the road toward the campground restrooms. Her head was down and her gait labored, whether because of their long hike, the encounter in the pie shop, or the argument was anybody's guess. Shortly after, her sister came out and stood, hands on hips, frowning at the surrounding area. When she noticed the Shoemaker group watching her, she turned and marched back into her little camper.

CHAPTER THREE
FRIDAY EVENING

"What do you suppose is going on?" Donna said.

"I would say one is sad and one is mad," Ben offered.

"Duh. That's obvious. But why?"

"It must have something to do with the guy in the pie shop," Frannie said. "They seemed fine before then."

"Maybe," said Jane Ann, "he is a relative and their great uncle died and left everything to him and one of the twins."

The rest just looked at her.

"*Could* be," she said and shrugged.

"So then why is one sad and not happy?" Ben asked.

"You have to figure some of this out for yourselves. I can't do all of the mental work around here," Jane Ann said.

"Metal work?" Mickey had been watching the little trailer.

"*Mental*! Like you, dear," she answered.

Larry got up. "I think it's time to clear the table." He started stacking the Shoemaker dishes while the others gathered their own.

Frannie followed Larry inside with a tray of condiments and the bowl of potato salad. As she covered the bowl and opened the refrigerator to wedge it in somewhere, she said, "I saw a sign by the campground office that they have fresh eggs. Think I'll walk over and pick some up for tomorrow morning. I forgot to bring any."

"We'll take the dogs for a walk. I think Ben wants to go over by that bird sanctuary."

"The dogs will like that," she answered with a grin.

"They will remain leashed, although I'm sure Cuba couldn't even catch a turtle any more."

Frannie grabbed her billfold and went outside. No one else was interested in accompanying her, so she debated riding her bike or walking, and decided to walk. The road led past several other campsites, all occupied, and then turned along the river. Laughter and cooking smells wafted across the road in the peaceful, early evening scene. The road turned again away from the river, along a few small campsites, to the shower house, restrooms, the large campground office and residence near the entrance.

In one of the sites, an old light blue pickup with a topper sat under a tree facing the road. Two people stood talking under a portable canopy. As Frannie neared, she realized it was one of the twins and the man from the pie shop. Their conversation wasn't audible but they leaned toward each other and their body language conveyed intense emotion. The woman appeared to have been crying. Curiouser and curiouser.

Frannie went on to the office and opened the screen door. A large woman stood behind the counter, with a round, rosy face and curly red hair pulled back by sizable rhinestone barrettes. Her lavender sweatshirt was embellished, Laverne-and-Shirley style, with a glittery 'MLL' monogram. She looked up from a ledger and beamed. A mottled gray cat with a white muzzle lay on the counter by the ledger.

"Welcome! Can I help you?" Her husky voice resembled Carol Channing's.

"Hi," Frannie said. "I saw your sign for fresh eggs?"

"You bet!" The woman actually guffawed, as she squeezed around the counter, although Frannie couldn't imagine what was so funny about eggs.

"Oof!" the woman said, having negotiated the narrow space. "Need to lose a few inches off these hips or we'll have to move the counter."

She opened an old refrigerator on the side wall. "How many?" she called from behind the door.

"Just a dozen," Frannie said. She reached out to stroke the cat. "What's your cat's name?"

"Phun."

"Fun?"

The woman stood up and closed the fridge. "Phun Munki." She spelled it. "My daughter has always loved sock monkeys. When we got the cat, she thought he resembled one, hence the name. But she was into creative spelling at the time."

As Frannie paid for the eggs, the woman said, "You're camping here right? That group on the second loop? Sites 75 to 78?"

Frannie thought a minute, marveling at the woman's memory when she couldn't remember her own site number so quickly. "Ummm, yeah—we're in 76, I think."

The woman thrust her hand across the counter. "I'm Mary Louise Larson. My husband has owned this place for almost thirty years. We got married last December—second time around for both of us. So now I'm in the campground business and lovin' it!"

Frannie nodded. "We've camped here before. It's a beautiful place."

"Anything else you need? We carry a few groceries and there's firewood in the bin outside."

"I believe my husband bought firewood earlier. Thanks!" Frannie turned to go.

"Any problems, you just holler," Mary Louise said and finished with her hearty laugh—one of those ha-ha-ha laughs that was so loud that it ought to be fake, but in Mary Louise's case, Frannie was sure it wasn't.

As Frannie passed the pickup-camper again, the blonde woman stepped onto the road, headed back to her own campsite.

Frannie smiled at her. "Nice evening."

The woman responded with a weak smile. "Yes, it is, I guess."

Frannie barged ahead as they continued down the road together. "I saw you walking earlier. Do you hike a lot?"

The woman nodded. "Virginia, my sister, and I live in Minneapolis so we go to a lot of trails around Minnesota." She paused a moment. "We're nature photographers too, so it's kind of a busman's holiday." She trudged along in silence, but Frannie wasn't giving up.

"We're from Iowa—here because we love the bike trail. Lots of other interesting places to visit, too. Is this your first time here?"

"No, we came here once before in the fall a couple of years ago."

"I bet it's really beautiful then. We keep saying we're going to but haven't done that yet," Frannie said.

The woman didn't reply, but let out a little sob and then caught herself. "I'm sorry," she said in a very faint voice. "I'm not myself. I've had quite a shock this afternoon."

Frannie turned. "I'm sorry to hear that. Is there... anything I can do?"

The woman shook her head. "It's done," she finally said.

"Val!" A male voice came from behind them. "Wait!" They both turned to see the man from the pickup loping up to them. Frannie said to the woman—Val apparently —"I'll see you later," and continued down the road, as slowly as she could without being obvious. However, she suspected the two behind her weren't much interested in her gait. She caught snatches of phrases—"start over—", "it's your life—," and "love you." Maybe Val's day was taking a turn for the better.

She glanced over her shoulder once to see the two locked in an embrace, and the man gently wiping Val's tears with a handkerchief. She smiled to herself. All's well that ends well.

When she returned to the campsite, she put the eggs and her billfold in the trailer and came back to where Jane Ann, Nancy, and Donna were sitting by the fire.

"Well, they aren't relatives," Frannie said, taking a chair.

"Who?" Jane Ann said, looking up from her magazine.

Frannie nodded toward the little trailer across the road. "The twins and the guy in the pie shop."

"How do you know?" Donna asked.

"Because one of the twins and the guy are in a clinch in the road back there whispering sweet nothings." She proceeded to fill them in on what she had learned. The others were making a few comments and speculations when Frannie shushed them because she noticed Val coming back up the road.

Val saw them sitting there and walked over. She nodded to the others and said to Frannie, "Could I talk to you a minute? In private?"

Frannie rose from her chair. "Sure. Why don't you come in our trailer?"

Val said to the other women, "I'm sorry for interrupting. Excuse us for a minute?" They all nodded, but Frannie could tell that Donna restrained herself with difficulty.

Inside, Frannie offered Val an iced tea and a seat, both of which she declined.

Instead, she leaned against the counter and took a deep breath. "I wanted to explain a little. I met Richard a few years ago on a cruise and we hit it off right away. But after I got home, something happened. Virginia, my sister, is very protective of me, and I guess she intervened. She does that, because people can't tell us apart so she met Richard pretending to be me and broke it off." She stopped and looked out the window toward her own trailer. "I hadn't seen or heard from him until today. I thought he lost interest. We are going to try and work it out, but we have to go slow with Virginia, get her used to the idea, so *please* don't say anything to her about what you saw or heard. She doesn't even know he's staying in this campground. On the cruise, Richard bought me a silver necklace with a Murano glass pendant and he just asked that I wear it while we're here so he knows it's me. I have to approach this very carefully." She finished with a pleading note in her voice.

"Certainly. Are you sure you don't want to sit down?"

"No, Virginia is already wondering where I am. I need to get back." She went to the door and turned. "Thank you. I don't even know your name."

"Frannie Shoemaker," Frannie smiled.

"I'm Valerie Peete." She surveyed the trailer and her eyes landed on a collage of old photos Frannie had hanging on the wall. She moved closer to examine them. Three children dressed in Indian gear looked seriously at the camera near a World War I era tent. "Great photos. Are they someone you know?"

Frannie smiled. "I'm not sure," she confessed. "My cousin found them in our grandmother's scrapbook. I think one of the boys is my dad but she doesn't think so. I just love the pictures."

"They are amazing," Valerie said. "Well, I'll see you around. Thanks again." She went out and continued to her own trailer, her step a little lighter.

Frannie poured herself a glass of pinot grigio and joined the women at the fire again. They watched her expectantly.

"Well?" Donna said.

Frannie shrugged and looked across the road at Val and Virginia's trailer. No sign of anyone.

"Where was I?" she asked the group.

"The clinch," Nancy said.

"Apparently, Val, the sister who was just here, was romantically involved a few years ago with Richard, the guy in the pie shop, and her sister, Virginia broke it up."

"Wow," said Donna. "The makings of a soap opera."

"How did she break it up?" Nancy asked.

"She pretended to be Val. That's all I know," Frannie said. "Here come the guys."

The men returned with the dogs and pulled their own chairs near the fire. They had their own stories.

"The campground is pretty full, even the tent area," Rob started.

"And we took that little path down to the river. There was a beaver working back and forth, getting reeds from the bank. He completely ignored us, even the dogs," Mickey added. "Ben took some great pictures on his phone."

"Really?" Nancy said. She considered the darkening sky. "It's probably getting too late to see him now."

Ben nodded. "But that's not all. Stuck back in the trees is a little old trailer, all closed up. Larry thinks it might be a meth lab or something."

"What?!?" Jane Ann sat forward.

Larry held up his hands. "Calm down. I only said it was a possibility. I'm sure the campground owners are very careful about that. It was suspicious because the windows were all covered from the inside with dark fabric or cardboard or something—not regular curtains or blinds. It's on the other side of a broken-down fence, so maybe it's not even on this property. We didn't see anything else or anyone hanging around there."

"Well, good," Nancy said, "because if it *is* something like that, they probably would have shot you all."

"And then, who would have driven all of these campers home?" Frannie said.

"Aww, your concern is touching," Mickey said.

Frannie noticed a golf cart coming along the road, stopping at each campsite. She recognized the driver as Mary Louise Larson by her wild curls, and the woman visited a few minutes with each group of campers who were outside. When she stopped even with Frannie's group, she called out, "How is everything this fine evening?"

"Great," Mickey yelled back.

"Who is that?" Donna whispered.

"One of the owners," Frannie said and got up from her chair. Nancy and Larry followed her out to the road.

"You folks need anything?" Mary Louise boomed and laughed.

"No, everything's fine," Frannie answered. She introduced Nancy, and then noticed the gray cat curled in the seat beside Mary Louise.

"Check out the cat, Nancy," she said and explained about the cat's name. Nancy was a diehard cat lover and walked around the cart so that she could pet him.

"He loves these rides every evening," Mary Louise said. "Hates the car and the truck but loves the golf cart. Go figure." She laughed again.

"He's beautiful," Nancy said, and as she stroked the cat, he purred and stretched.

"He likes you!" Mary Louise said.

"All cats like Nancy," Frannie told her.

Larry asked Mary Louise about the trailer the men had seen on the other side of the campground. She frowned, the first time Frannie had seen her without her broad smile.

"That's Mel Dubrak. He's not on our land. He's kind of a pain but doesn't do any harm. He uses our road, and my husband even caught him using the shower house." She wrinkled her nose and then laughed again. "Not that he didn't need it!"

"You don't think there's any possibility that he's making meth there?" Larry asked.

Mary Louise shrugged and sighed. "I know the cops have been trying to find a source that they are sure is in this area and they suspect him. But I really don't think so. He tries hard with his son, Dale, and believe me, that kid is a trial! Never have seen *him* smile."

Drawn by Mary Louise's booming voice, the twins appeared around the corner of their trailer.

"Looka here," Mary Louise fairly shouted. "It's Peete and Repeat!" She rocked the cart laughing at her own joke.

They were both smiling and more relaxed than earlier as they walked up to the cart.

"I call 'em the campground paparazzi," Mary Louise told the others. "They're always snapping those fancy cameras."

The twins laughed, and one of them—who knew which?—said, "Just nature photos, Mary Louise. We don't take pictures of any of your famous guests."

"Right," Mary Louise laughed. "This place is *full* of celebrities."

Larry told them about the beaver that the men had recently spotted on the riverbank.

"We saw him this morning," the other twin said. "Got some great shots of him. There's wonderful wildflowers in that area too."

Mary Louise put the cart in gear. "Well, I'd best finish my rounds. You folks have a nice night!" They all stepped away from the cart as she sped off toward the next group of sites.

Nancy wasn't about to let the twins go. "Come and join us for a beverage. I'd love to hear about your photography. "

One said, "Sure, for a few minutes." Frannie remembered a Halloween years before when friends showed up completely disguised, and how disconcerting it is to talk to someone when you have no idea who it is.

However, the suspense was short-lived. The woman continued, "I'm Virginia Peete, by the way, and this is my sister Valerie."

As they walked back to the fire and completed introductions, Frannie tried to spot some differentiating characteristic that would allow her to keep them straight, but was stymied. Their hair, glasses, physical shape and size and clothing were identical. Mirror images—wait a minute—they *are* mirror images, she thought. Virginia wore a watch on her right wrist, Valerie on her left. Virginia must be left-handed. That solved, Frannie relaxed and listened to the conversation.

"We're professional free-lance photographers, mostly nature and scenery," Virginia was saying.

"We sell to magazines, calendar companies, writers doing nature books...," Valerie added but Virginia jumped in.

"Not so many for books, but this week we've spent a lot of time at the nature center, shooting some of the environmental classes. Have you been over there? We got some great shots of the high ropes course. Mostly we do greeting cards and stationery, notecards, calendars, that kind of thing. That's why we were working down by the river this morning."

"The wildflowers are just...," Valerie started, but Virginia leaned forward in her chair and interrupted again.

"There's a very odd little old trailer back there that we took some shots of — kind of a scruffy-looking guy hanging around. He didn't look very happy about us taking pictures."

"He saw you taking pictures?" Larry asked.

"I assume so — he watched us the whole time," Virginia said, unconcerned. "I think we can get a great black-and-white photo spread out of it. There was an old pickup there too that really added to the ambience."

"I think you should be careful about that ambience," Larry said. "They may be doing something illegal there. We were just asking Mary Louise about it."

"What do you mean?" Valerie asked.

"They aren't actually on the campground land, but I just thought it looked suspicious and would be careful, if I were you," Larry repeated.

"Larry used to be a cop," Mickey said. "He's suspicious of everybody."

Larry frowned. "This may not be a joking matter, Mick."

"I know, I know," Mickey's grin disappeared and he held up his hands.

"We're fascinated by your trailer," Nancy said.

"It's German," Virginia said. "We saw them when we were traveling in Europe a couple of years ago and had one shipped back. Since we do a lot of our work in state and national parks, camping is the best way to go and we love it."

Nancy said, "Do you both pull it or...".

"I drive," Virginia said. "Valerie really doesn't want to." Valerie didn't say anything.

The conversation continued around the places the twins had camped with Virginia doing most of the talking and Valerie adding small embellishments. Virginia was describing a hike along the south shore of Lake Superior when Valerie grabbed her hand.

"Ginny," she said. "There's that pickup."

"Don't call me that," Virginia growled, but she followed her sister's gaze, as did the rest of the group. An old rusty gray truck rattled slowly along the main campground road. A man in the passenger seat, elbow out the open window, surveyed the campground and seemed to fixate on them, although he was some distance away. Frannie thought the description 'scruffy' was probably too kind. They couldn't see the driver.

Finally, Valerie said, "So what kinds of places do you guys camp?" Virginia looked a little put out at losing the center of the stage.

After listening impatiently a few minutes, Virginia said, "Valerie, if we're going to get that walk in, we'd better get going."

Valerie nodded and got up. Mickey said, "Another hike? How many miles have you already put on today?"

Virginia laughed. "Just a turn around the campground before bed. We're early risers." They left and headed along the road, away from the entrance.

As they disappeared, Frannie said, "Very odd. I can see the fascination with dressing alike when twins are children, but as adults?"

Jane Ann agreed. "How would you even know which one you were by that time?"

Mickey looked at his wife, puzzled. "What?"

"I mean, you would have no sense of individual identity, I would think."

Nancy suggested a trip to the nature center the next morning. "There's actually an old path from here along the river if we want to hike it. A little hilly, but not bad."

"We'll meet you there, Nance," Mickey said, and the rest agreed, laughing. Nancy was much more eager for physical activity than the others. After discussing the logistics and confirming a good weather forecast, they retired to their units for the night.

Chapter Four

Early Saturday Morning

Virginia climbed out of her bottom bunk and pulled on a sweatshirt. She put a cup of water in the microwave for tea and, while waiting for it to heat, peered out the window, stretching her back. A faint chirp came from Valerie's windbreaker on the dinette seat. She glanced back to make sure the curtain to the bedroom was closed, and pulled Valerie's cell out of the jacket pocket. A text message from Richard.

"Old Power Plant at 9:30. Wear your necklace."

As she deleted the message and replaced the phone, she thought, "Necklace?" Then she remembered a silver chain with a pinkish Murano glass pendant that Valerie said she had gotten at one of the ports of call on the cruise and wore on special occasions. It had made Virginia angry at the time that Valerie hadn't bought her one like it; they *always* did that for each other. So. It must have been a gift from Richard.

She sat down at the dinette with her tea and looked at her watch. 7:30. They had hiked to the old power plant before; Valerie must have met Richard secretly and mentioned it to him. Somehow, she needed to get away without Valerie. They had planned to get some photos this morning in a wildlife sanctuary on the other side of Burdensville.

Soon she heard Valerie clamber out of the top bunk. "Good morning!" her sister said cheerily, pulling back the curtain on the bedroom entrance. She was dressed in the same pajamas and sweatshirt as her twin and looked more upbeat than any time since the pie shop yesterday. Something was definitely up.

Virginia spoke weakly. "I don't know how good. I'm afraid I've caught something." She looked up with a drawn face.

Valerie was immediately concerned. "Oh, no. Upset stomach or what?"

"Just dizzy and chills." She shivered. "I don't know if I should go traipse around that sanctuary this morning."

"Don't worry about it. We've got time; we can go later." Valerie started fixing her own tea.

"But it's such a beautiful morning. What if the weather changes? Maybe you should go and get some shots while the light is good."

Virginia could see surprise and then comprehension of this sudden freedom on Valerie's face.

"Well,...I could. Are you sure you'll be okay?"

"I think I'll just try and get some more sleep. I'll be fine."

"Can I fix you something to eat?"

"Not right now. Nothing sounds good." Virginia made a face.

"Okay. Maybe I'll go shower then."

After Valerie had gathered her supplies and left the trailer for the shower house, Virginia went back to the bedroom and found Valerie's small travel jewelry pouch. She spotted the Murano necklace right on top, untangled it from the rest, and stuck it in the pocket of her sweatshirt. By the time Valerie returned, she was back at the dinette.

Valerie went into the tiny half-bath to dry her hair and put on makeup, spending more time than she normally would for a trek through a wildlife sanctuary. Then Virginia could hear her in the bedroom rummaging through the jewelry pouch.

"Virginia?" she called, "Have you seen my necklace? The one I got on the cruise?"

Virginia smiled to herself. "Oh, yeah! I found it on the floor of the kitchen before we left home. I laid it on the kitchen counter. Didn't you see it?"

"No." Valerie sounded crushed.

"Well, you don't need it this morning, do you?" Virginia couldn't resist.

Valerie came out of the bedroom. "No, of course not." But she didn't sound convincing. She wore jeans, a white tank top and open denim shirt with a long blue plaid scarf loosely tied. After loading up her camera bag, she slung it over her shoulder and grabbed her cell phone out of her jacket pocket, her cowboy hat and the truck keys.

"Call me if you get to feeling worse," she said.

"I will."

Virginia heard the little pickup start and pull out. She got up and rummaged through her storage compartment for a matching outfit to Val's attire. No time for a shower; she did a little extra work on her hair to get it just right and fastened on Valerie's necklace. Finally, she pulled a small backpack from under the dinette bench and put in a water bottle and a couple of granola bars. Her small Ruger LCR revolver already nestled in the bottom of the bag.

The trail to the nature center and the power plant started on the far side of the campground, so after locking the camper, she took off along the back road to the trailhead. It was just 8:30, so she would have plenty of time to get to the power plant for the date with Richard.

Valerie drove toward Burdensville, enjoying the sparkling morning. Traffic was heavier than she expected for a Saturday, but there was a farmers' market that morning which probably explained it. Shortly after passing through Burdensville, she pulled into the wildlife sanctuary and parked. Before getting out of the truck, she dialed Richard on her cell. According to the dashboard clock, it was 9:00 and he should be up. There had been no sign of him when she passed his camper on her way to the shower.

He answered at once. Her heart lifted just hearing his voice. Everything *would* work out.

"Good morning!" she said. "Virginia isn't feeling well this morning so I'm out on my own. Can we meet somewhere?"

There was a pause. "Didn't you get my text?"

"Oh, sorry, I didn't even check for messages this morning. What about?"

He told her about his suggested rendezvous.

"I can make that! I'll just come back here later and get some shots so I have something to show Virginia for my morning." She giggled.

"Great! I'll see you there."

She hung up and checked her messages. Nothing from Richard. Reception wasn't great in the campground; the message would probably show up sometime this afternoon. She just wished she had her necklace. She started the truck, pulled out of the parking lot, and headed back to the nature center.

Virginia made good time on the trail and, shortly before it ended at the nature center parking lot, took a little-used cutoff that led down to the old power plant. The way was steep and narrow, beset by roots, overgrowth, and rock outcroppings. The hulking building built into the side of the cliff had a gaping entry at the upper level. Doors and windows were long gone, and the floor on that level was weak and broken in places. Rusty beams hung down from the remains of the ceiling like bony fingers. A narrow staircase along the back wall led down to the lower level which had a cement floor. Trees and shrubs poked in at the open windows, and busted pipes and trash covered the floor surrounding rusted derelicts of machinery that filled the center of the room. Not exactly a place for a romantic tryst in Virginia's opinion. One more strike against Richard.

She picked her way halfway around the room to an open doorway that led into a smaller room. The floor was in better shape in here and she stood for a moment at a window overlooking the river, sparkling and dancing on its way to the Mississippi. She looked at her watch. 9:15. Richard should be here soon. She considered their situation. She and Valerie had, practically speaking, lived together their whole lives. In their twenties, they had tried marriage to another set of identical twins, Dan and Ron Flack, whom they had met at a twins' convention. A double wedding, followed by a shared duplex. It was pleasant, but Virginia could tell that Valerie wasn't happy. Virginia's husband, Dan was an okay guy but not any great catch. So three years later, they both filed for divorce and had lived together ever since.

They had a full life—rewarding work, a very nice home, travel, and friends who provided a social life whenever they wanted it. Money was no issue; their parents' deaths a couple of years before had left them extremely well off and able to quit their day jobs to concentrate on their photography full time. But Valerie was such a sucker for almost any guy who looked her way and there were plenty of fortune hunters out there. This wasn't the first time Virginia had had to intervene, but Richard proved more persistent.

She fingered the glass stone on the chain at her neck and heard someone on the stairs. Footsteps crossed the floor of the other room.

She unzipped her backpack and set it on the floor just inside the door and walked through, expecting to see Richard. Instead, Valerie rounded the corner of the old machinery. They both registered the same shocked expression. Time seemed to stop as each woman realized the implications of the other one's presence.

Virginia said, "Valerie! But—"

Valerie's eyes were drawn to her sister's hand clasping the pendant, and all the heartbreak of the last four years exploded as she lashed out. "*My* necklace! I thought you hadn't seen it! And I thought you were *sick!*" With each word that she hissed, she moved closer into Virginia's face. Virginia started to back up.

"No—"

"No what?" Valerie's voice got even higher and more menacing. "You pretended you were me and broke it off with Richard once and now you're trying to do it again. I *had* to marry Ron so that you could marry Dan." She exploded and screamed, "You cannot stand for me to have a life of my own!"

Valerie's shrill voice covered up the scuffing sound of more footsteps coming from the opposite corner of the room.

CHAPTER FIVE

SATURDAY MORNING

Larry pulled their pickup into the nature center parking lot.

"Quite a few cars already," he commented.

The parking lot was ringed on three sides by large Prairie-style buildings. The largest, in the middle, had a "Visitor Center" sign, so they headed that way.

"Wow. This looks like a pretty big operation," Mickey said, looking around.

"It's actually an environmental learning center," Nancy said. "They have all kinds of programs — day camps, weekend programs for families, corporate and school programs, some just for women. There's a high ropes course that you might want to try, Mickey." She grinned at him.

"Uh, I'll get back to you on that."

They went in the main entrance and stood looking around.

"Help you?" A young, no-nonsense looking woman stood staunchly behind a desk, clad in a crisp green uniform with an engraved badge reading 'Deborah McCabe.'

"We just want to look around," Larry said. "Do you have brochures or maps or something?"

She took one brochure off a stack and laid it smartly in front of him. "Our main mission is intensive *participation* programs for both children and adults. We offer programs for schools, families and corporate retreats. We also have volunteering opportunities, if you are interested in that." She paused and then continued reluctantly. "We do have exhibits in this building that you are welcome to look at. There is no charge but we *do* encourage donations." She nodded at a clear acrylic box on the counter with a slit in the top and half-filled with fives and tens.

Larry said, "Yes, ma'am," and dropped a couple of bills in the box.

As they walked away, Frannie chuckled. "You are as much of a smartass as me."

"I was not being smart. She reminds me of my fifth grade teacher, Miss Budlong. Except Miss Budlong was much older. But no way I would mess with either of them."

The others made their contributions and followed. They browsed the small exhibit of plants and wildlife and dioramas of the region.

As they circled back to the entrance, Frannie said, "Just a minute," and walked back over to the information counter.

Deborah McCabe looked up, disappointed when she saw Frannie again, meaning no large reservations, volunteers, or big donations were forthcoming. "Yes?"

"Aren't there some hiking trails too?" Frannie asked.

"Yes, there are." Deborah stood there, stoic.

"Well, do you have a map of those trails?" Frannie asked, as sweetly as possible.

"Yes, we do," and she grabbed a trifold off another stack and laid it in front of Frannie, who wasn't about to be frightened off.

"Is there a trail that leads down to that old power plant?"

"There is, but it isn't safe, and neither it nor the power plant are on our property. We are not liable for them."

"I understand. Where is that trail?"

Deborah McCabe gave a loud sigh. "It's off the trail that goes down to the River Bend Campground." She pointed in the general direction, and returned to her ledger. "Now if you'll excuse me…"

"Certainly. Thank you for *all* of your help," Frannie said with a straight face and turned back to her friends, rolling her eyes.

Back outside, after a short conference, Frannie, Donna, Nancy, and Ben decided to try the path down to the power plant and the others opted to check out the high ropes course.

"Not that I plan to try it," Mickey assured them. "Just want to see what it's about."

"I see there's a session this afternoon," Ben said. "I think I'll try it then."

"If you don't fall in a hole in the power plant," Jane Ann said.

They split up and Frannie's group found the cutoff after passing it only once. Ben led and pointed out tricky footing spots as they gingerly descended into the thick woods and undergrowth. They could make out the shape of the old building through the trees and finally gathered on a small slab at the entrance. In spite of the sun filtering through the trees, the massive relic squatted threateningly.

Nancy entered the opening and gaped at the busted floor and ceiling, bristling with twisted beams.

"Looks like maybe this is far as we go," she said.

"No, look! There's a stairway here," Donna said. She was the last one in and stood in the open doorway pointing down to the right. The stairs were cement and looked sturdy, so she started down hugging the wall. Frannie looked at the others, shrugged and went after her. Ben and Nancy followed. When they reached the lower level, they looked around at the large rusted machinery filling the center of the room and debris on the floor. Sunlit trees could be glimpsed through the window openings, but a deep gloomy chill pervaded the room.

"I'll bet there's a great view of the river from those windows," Donna said, picking her way through the clutter. Frannie was nervous about letting Donna lead; they would be lucky if they didn't end up hauling her out by a medevac helicopter.

Donna only tripped once, and managed to make her way pretty quickly to the end of the machinery. She looked back at them, saying, "At least the floor is solid here," and rounded the corner.

She stopped. She gasped for breath and made a mewling sound.

The others halted too, looking at each other in confusion. Donna hadn't fallen; she stood frozen in place, staring at the floor in front of her.

"Is the floor gone?" Ben asked from behind Frannie.

Donna looked back again, her face colorless. She shook her head.

"There's two bodies. It's those twins." She spoke slowly and quietly, not typical for Donna.

They moved up beside her and saw the carnage on the floor. One of the women lay on her side with her head wedged in the machinery, a gaping wound on the side of her head that had bled profusely. Her sister lay next to her, face up, her skin a sickly grey-blue. Ben sidled around Donna and bent to check the pulse of the woman on her back.

He straightened. "No pulse. She's still warm though so this must have just happened."

Donna's eyes grew wider still as she looked around. "You mean the murderer might still be here?" she croaked.

"Could they have killed each other?" Frannie asked.

"I have no idea," Ben said. "I think we need to go back upstairs—I doubt if phones will work here—and you can go back up and get help. I'll stay here."

"I'll stay with you," Nancy said. "The murderer *could* be nearby."

"And you're going to protect me?" Ben gave a little smile at his wife.

"Someone has to," Nancy answered, and Frannie suspected that Nancy, small and wiry and very fit, could hold her own.

She led Donna back up the stairs and out to the path.

"Do you think they'll be okay?" Donna asked, puffing along behind Frannie.

"*If* someone else killed those women, and I'm not so sure of that, both deaths look like crimes of passion — not planned. I don't think the murderer would hang around. Besides, Ben can take care of himself." Ben worked out daily and had considerable upper body strength.

They trudged on up the path.

"You don't think someone else killed them?" Donna said, panting.

"They were having some issues. Maybe it was a murder-suicide or something. Depends on how they died."

They reached the parking lot and Frannie debated calling 911, but also felt they needed to notify the nature center first and let them take charge. She wished Larry was around but there was no sign of him or the rest of their group. He would know what to do.

Reluctantly she led the way over to the Visitor's Center. The only Center employee that they saw when the entered was Deborah McCabe at the information desk. Frannie hurried over to her.

"Ma'am?"

Deborah McCabe looked up and frowned when she saw Frannie. "What is it?" So much for customer service.

"We hiked down to the power plant and there are two dead women down there. I wonder if you could call the authorities?"

Deborah did not flinch. "As I told you, we have no liability there. That is not Center property. Don't you have a cell phone? You need to call 911."

Frannie stammered. "Yes, I do, but I thought…"

"Is there a problem here?" A pudgy man, also in a green uniform, had come out of an office behind Deborah McCabe.

Frannie explained the situation, with Donna adding embellishments. The man registered much more reaction than McCabe.

"Let me get this straight. *Two* dead bodies? Are you sure? Follow me." Without waiting for any answers, he turned and marched back in to the office.

Frannie resisted smirking at McCabe as she and Donna rounded the counter and walked into a compulsively neat office.

The man hurried around the desk and pulled the phone toward him but did not sit down. He dialed, and when it was picked up said, "Yes, this is Director Lindorf at the Nature Center. We have just had a report of two dead women down in the old power plant." He paused. "No, it doesn't appear to be an accident." He raised his eyebrows at Frannie and she nodded. "Thanks. Yes, they're here. We'll wait for you in the parking lot." He hung up.

He came around the desk again and motioned for Frannie and Donna to follow him. As they passed the information desk, he said over his shoulder, "Deborah, we'll be outside waiting for the sheriff."

"But Bob, you have a meeting in ten minutes with…"

"Tell them we'll have to reschedule," and he headed out the door. Outside, he stood where he could see the entrance drive and turned to the two women.

"Were you alone when you discovered the—?"

Frannie said, "No, there were two other friends with us. They waited there."

He frowned. "That could be dangerous. We need to get back down there as fast as possible. As soon as the authorities arrive."

They stood in silence for a moment. There was little wind and a few lazy bugs circled them. A perfect early summer day. Laughter reached them from one of the other hiking paths. Larry and the rest of Frannie's group emerged from the trees on the other side of the parking lot.

"Larry!" Frannie shouted, and motioned them over. When they arrived, Larry looked at the Director standing by Frannie.

"What's the matter?"

Frannie told him what they found in the power plant. They all talked at once.

"Those women next to us?" Rob said. Like they had run in to a lot of twins that weekend.

"Are you sure they're dead?" Jane Ann asked.

"Ben and Nancy are still there?" said Larry.

"What are we waiting for?" Mickey wanted to know.

In answer to his question, a sheriff's car pulled into the entrance.

A petite woman with short brown curls jumped out of the car almost before it came to a stop. As she approached, Lindorf mumbled to Frannie, "Don't let her size fool you."

"What's going on, Bob?" she asked, jogging up to the group.

Director Lindorf introduced her to the group as Sheriff Mary Sorenson and precisely recounted the events.

"The paramedics are on their way, although sounds like it's probably too late. Which of you actually found the body?"

Donna and Frannie raised their hands. The sheriff jotted down their names and hometown. Frannie gave her Ben and Nancy's names as well.

"Did you touch anything? Move anything?"

"Ben checked for a pulse—he's a physical therapist," Frannie said. As if no one else was qualified to take a pulse.

"Okay, I need to get down there. I would like one of the women who discovered the bodies to go with me."

Donna usually had to be in the middle of everything, but paled, stepped back, and said, "Frannie can go."

Frannie said, "Can my husband come, too? He's a retired cop," and then thought she sounded like a five-year-old, begging for a friend to go on a family outing. The sheriff looked at the rest of the group and Larry stepped forward a half step and raised his hand slightly.

The sheriff appraised him a moment and then said, "Good idea. Let's go."

They had a little trouble keeping up with Sorenson. When they reached the power plant, Frannie introduced Ben and Nancy and indicated the stairway to the lower level. Sheriff Sorenson sent the Terells back to the nature center and led the way down the narrow cement steps. When they got to the bottom, Frannie pointed out the direction to go around the machinery. As the sheriff picked her way through the debris, Frannie noticed that the place seemed to have acquired an even more sinister air, just because she knew what lay on the other side of the room.

She watched the sheriff as the woman turned the corner. A little look of shock before her face turned impassive. Frannie and Larry reached the corner, but stood back while the sheriff examined the bodies. When Sorenson stood, she noticed the open door to the second room, and, resting a hand on the gun at her side, sidled around the bodies, and peeked around the edge of the door.

She relaxed when she saw no threat there, but before turning around, she glanced down at the floor, and pulling a pen out of her shirt pocket, leaned around the corner and snagged a small backpack by the strap.

She held it up for Frannie to see and said, "Did you see this here before?"

"No. None of us went in there," Frannie said.

Sorenson carefully replaced the bag where she found it.

"So you know these women?"

"We just met them last night," Larry said. "They're camped across the road from us at River Bend."

"What are their names?"

"Valerie and Virginia Peete," Frannie said. The horror of the site began to harden into a lump in her stomach. "I think they're—that is, they were—from Minneapolis. The campground owners should have that information."

"Do you know which one's which?" Sorenson asked.

Larry and Frannie both shook their heads, then Frannie said, "Wait!" and looked at their wrists. The woman who had fallen into the machinery had a watch on her right wrist; the other woman wasn't wearing one. She pointed at the one with the watch. "I think that's Virginia."

But then she noticed something else. "Can I move a little closer?" she asked the sheriff. Sorenson nodded and moved into the open doorway so that Frannie could get past her. Frannie bent over the woman, trying to ignore the bloody wound to her head. Fastened around her neck was a necklace such as Valerie had described to her the night before.

She straightened. "I don't know for sure. I think that necklace belongs to Valerie. But..." She continued to stare, noticing the clasp exposed at the back of the woman's neck as she lay on her side, her hair falling away.

She turned to the sheriff to explain her dilemma. "Last night, the one who introduced herself as Virginia wore her watch on her right wrist, so I thought she must be left-handed. Valerie wore hers on her left. I was trying to figure out some way to tell them apart. But Valerie had told me about that necklace earlier—said she had gotten it from a man she was in love with. He's at the campground this weekend and asked her to wear it."

She shook her head. "*But*, the thing is, it looks like the necklace was fastened by a left-handed person." Frannie looked from the sheriff to her husband.

"What are you talking about?" he said.

She looked back at the sheriff. "You know what I mean. If you are right-handed, you work the little clasp-thingy with your right hand and hook it into the little ring on the left. That necklace has the clasp thingy on the left, so it looks like she is left-handed and that *is* Virginia. But she seems to be wearing Valerie's necklace."

Larry still looked baffled, but Mary Sorenson nodded. "I see. Very observant. I didn't find any ID on them. We'll hope there's something in their dental records, because if they *are* identical twins, DNA won't be any help. If their fingerprints are in the system, we can use those."

"You don't think they're identical?" Frannie asked.

"Well, fraternal twins can look a lot alike, but these two appear to be identical. We'll see."

"They told us they had been to Europe so they should have passports on record."

"You're right. Thank you for your help," the sheriff said as they all heard more footsteps on the stairs. "I'll want to talk to you later. Try to remember if they felt threatened by anyone. You're staying at River Bend, right?"

Larry nodded and gave her their site number. He and Frannie moved into the corner to allow the EMTs to pass and then went back up the stairs. As they headed back up to the parking lot, they met an older man carrying a bag and a young one in a sheriff's department jacket. They nodded at Larry and Frannie and took the path down to the power plant.

"Must be the medical examiner and a crime scene tech," Larry said.

When they rejoined their group, questions flew. Donna, as usual, led the bombardment.

"What did the sheriff say? Did she think it was murder?"

"She didn't share—just asked us what we knew about them," Larry said.

"Do we need to stay here?" Mickey asked.

"They're definitely dead?" Jane Ann said.

Larry held his hands up. "We really don't know anything more. The sheriff said she'd come talk to us later, so we might as well head back to the campground." It was a quiet ride back.

CHAPTER SIX

LATE SATURDAY MORNING

When they arrived back at the campground, Frannie noticed that the old blue pickup with the topper was parked in the same spot. She would have to make sure the sheriff gave Richard the news. She certainly didn't want to do it. Back at their campsites, Mickey put on a new pot of coffee.

As they settled in their chairs, Jane Ann said, "Do you suppose we're going to be confined to the campground again?" She was referring to two previous incidents in their camping history when that very thing had happened.

"I doubt it very much," Larry said. "This time the crime wasn't committed here and there's no reason to believe it was one of the campers any more than an outsider."

"I heard that people all over the Midwest are checking to make sure Frannie doesn't have the next campsite when they make their reservations these days," Mickey said, grinning.

"Oh, hush," Frannie said. "You and Jane Ann were there both times too."

"And people have avoided being next to Mickey for years," Larry added.

"Seriously, Larry, could you tell anything about how they died?" Nancy said.

"Of course, that will be determined by the medical examiner, but on the surface it appeared that the one was pushed into that machinery and the other may have been choked or strangled, judging from the tone of her skin."

"Which one was which?" Donna asked.

Frannie shrugged and told the group what they had observed. She also repeated what Valerie had told her the night before about the necklace.

"From what she said, it sounded like Virginia had impersonated her in order to break her up with Richard."

"Could they have killed each other?" Ben asked Larry.

"I don't see how."

"Wonder if that guy Richard knows yet," Donna said.

Frannie thought about him. "He's camping here—I saw his truck when we pulled in. But the authorities wouldn't have any reason to notify him. The sheriff didn't find any ID so they wouldn't know *who* to notify."

Nancy said, "Neither of them had a purse or anything?"

That jogged something in Frannie's memory. "The sheriff found a little backpack on the floor in other room. But...I saw one of them leave this morning in the pickup and she had a camera bag. I didn't see that there."

"But if only one went in the pickup, how did the other one get to the power plant?" Rob said.

"The hiking path," Nancy said.

"But that would be odd," Frannie said. "If they were both going to end up in the same place, why didn't they go together?"

Larry said to Frannie, "You're sure only one was in the truck?"

Frannie nodded. "She waved before she got in the truck. It was about 8:30—we were done with breakfast and the rest of you were inside, I think."

They sat in silence for a few minutes. Then Larry rubbed his hand over his crewcut and leaned forward in his chair, elbows on knees and hands clasped. "I'm still worried about that old trailer. Those women were photographing it yesterday and they said one of the guys saw them."

"If one of them took the hiking path," Nancy said, "it's on that side of the campground. She might have been seen by one of those guys."

Larry nodded and sat back. "Well, the sheriff said she wanted to talk to us and would be over. We need to tell her about the camera bag, the guys in the old trailer, and you need to fill her in on Richard. Did you say he's camped here, too?" He looked at Frannie.

"Yeah, his site is over near the office. He has a little blue pickup with a topper. It was there when we came back just now."

Donna got out the cinnamon rolls left from breakfast and coffee mugs were refilled. Conversation rambled in kind of an audible version of shuffling feet and twiddling thumbs.

When the sheriff's car edged up the road, everyone perked up, hoping for an end to the suspenseful atmosphere.

Mary Sorenson parked her patrol car on the grassy edge of the road and pulled a small notebook out of her pocket as she walked toward them. She declined coffee but accepted a lawn chair.

"I'm going to go back in a minute and have you tell me everything you know about these women, but when you first went down to the power plant, did you meet anyone?"

The ones who had made that hike all shook their heads. "No, we didn't," Ben said.

"And you," she looked at Ben, "stayed there while the others went for help? Did you see or hear anyone while you waited?"

"Not a soul," Ben said. "Why?"

Sorenson sighed. "From the preliminary ME's examination, it appears they must have died about 9:30."

Nancy's mouth dropped open. "But, that's just about the time we started down there!"

Frannie nodded. "We got to the Visitor's Center right after it opened and looked around at the exhibits, then split up to explore." She shivered. "But we didn't see anyone on our way down there."

"We got the call about 9:55," Sorenson said.

"And you think they were definitely killed by someone else?" Frannie said.

"There had to have been someone else involved," Sorenson said.

"Could they have left by the river?" Rob asked.

"It's possible but seems unlikely. At least if it was a premeditated murder. The murderer would have had to come by canoe, and it would be pretty hard to time their arrival. Maybe a spontaneous thing; the fact that they were killed by different methods points to that...like a robbery gone bad. We didn't find a purse or wallet on either of them." She shifted in her chair.

"What about that backpack? Anything in there?" Frannie asked.

Sorenson shook her head. "No ID. Now tell me how you met these women."

They took turns filling the sheriff in on their observations of the twins on the path and the incident in the pie shop. Frannie described her first conversation with Valerie on the road and later in the camper.

"Then last night," Larry said, "we visited with them for a while and they said they had taken some photos of animals and wildflowers over by the river, but also of that derelict trailer that sits next to the campground property. They thought it was 'interesting,' but I have to wonder if it isn't a meth lab or something."

Mary Sorenson nodded. "We've suspected that place for a month or more but haven't been able to catch them at anything. Did you see either of the women this morning?"

"I did," Frannie said. "One of them left in their truck about 8:30. She had a camera bag with her."

"Only one?" Mary Sorenson thought a moment. "She must have come back to get her sister?"

Frannie shook her head. "I don't see how she could have. We would have met her—there's only one way out of the campground, and from here to the nature center without going miles out of your way. Given the time frame, we think the other twin must have hiked the trail to the power plant."

Mary Sorenson frowned. "Why do you suppose they would have gone separately if they were going the same place? You didn't talk to either of them this morning?"

"No. We wondered the same thing. Maybe one of them wanted to hike and the other didn't."

"Could be something that simple, I suppose."

"Did you find a camera bag?" Frannie asked.

The sheriff shook her head. "Not in the power plant or in their truck." She stood. "Mary Louise said their camper is across from you?"

Donna pointed out the unique vehicle. "Over there next to ours."

The sheriff pulled a set of keys out of her pocket. "These were in the backpack. I'm hoping one of them opens the trailer."

Larry pointed to one on the ring. "Probably that one."

Sorenson thanked them and headed across the road.

"I wanted to see inside that thing," Donna said. "I hoped the twins would give us a tour today."

Rob frowned. "Not going to happen, honey."

"Well, I know that *now*. I just meant..."

"I know...just pulling your chain."

The sheriff gained entrance and a few minutes later, appeared back in the road.

"Ms. Shoemaker?"

"Yes?" Frannie got up and walked toward her.

"There are a couple of purses in the trailer. Would you take a look and see if you recognize them?"

"Sure." Frannie followed her back to the camper. "But I don't think we ever saw either of them with a purse." She gloated a little knowing Donna was sitting back there stewing because Frannie was going to get inside.

The interior of the little trailer was very streamlined and modern — kind of minimalist. Plain white cabinets in the tiny kitchen area were bracketed with natural wood. The ends were filled with bunk beds in the back and a built-in dinette in the front, all brightly lit by a large skylight. No clutter marred the interior, except for two matching tapestry bags sitting on the table.

"Is that where you found them?" Frannie asked the sheriff.

"No, one was in the storage under the dinette bench and the other in a bin of clothes under the bunk bed. I take it you haven't seen them before?"

Frannie shook her head. "When we saw them on the trail, they had matching fanny packs on. Then later when we talked to them, they weren't carrying anything."

"Hmmm. Fanny packs. I didn't find billfolds or any ID in the purses. Maybe they're in the fanny packs." She started opening cabinets and drawers. From an overhead cabinet near the door, she pulled two black fanny packs. Unzipping them, she pulled a billfold out of each, nodded, and replaced them.

"This is what we were looking for. I'll take them and the purses with me. Thanks for your help."

Frannie took the hint and headed out the door, followed by the sheriff. Sorenson relocked the door and, as they walk back to the campsite, questioned Frannie about her hometown and camping experiences. Frannie left out the parts about the previous murders and abduction.

As she approached her car, Mary Sorenson asked, "Do you know this Richard's last name?"

"No, — Valerie never said."

"But he's in a small blue pickup camper over near the office?"

"Yes," Frannie said. "It'll be on your left shortly before you get to the office."

"Mary Louise will be able to give me that info then. Thanks for all your help." The sheriff shook Frannie's hand, got back in her cruiser, and left.

When Frannie returned to her group, they were deep in the throes of a discussion planning their afternoon.

"I saw she found their purses," Donna said. "What's the trailer like?"

"Yeah, the purses and their fanny packs. The camper is really cool—kind of Scandinavian looking. Clean lines, light colors."

"I found the company on the internet," Mickey said. "They are *neat*."

"We're talking about what to do this afternoon," Larry said. "Ben and Nancy want to go back to the nature center and try the high ropes course."

"Um—that would be a 'no' for me." Frannie plopped in her chair.

"Me either," Donna said. "I think Rob's going to take me back into Burdensville to check out more shops. Want to come?" Rob did not look overly excited about the prospect.

"I don't know…What are you guys doing, Jane Ann?"

"We're thinking about a canoe float," Jane Ann offered. "There's a two hour one at 1:00—they run a shuttle from here."

"That's a nice float. Larry and I did it several years ago when we were here by ourselves."

"Interested in doing it again?" Larry asked her.

"Sure," Frannie said. No way she was going to do the high ropes course and a lazy afternoon drifting down the river beat following Donna, an Olympic shopping contender, from store to store hands down.

Rob looked at his wife. "Sure you don't want to do the float? Save the shopping for a later day?"

Donna pouted. "Quite a few of them aren't open on Mondays. And tomorrow we were going to take the bikes out to Wheat Valley and do that part of the trail."

"No problem." Rob was used to catering. "We'll do the float another time."

That settled, Mickey and Larry biked up to the office to reserve canoes for the 1:00 float, while the others got lunch fixings out. When Mickey and Larry returned, they reported that the sheriff's car was still at Richard's campsite.

71

CHAPTER SEVEN

EARLY SATURDAY AFTERNOON

After lunch, Frannie changed into shorts and a loose shirt, and gathered sunscreen, a visor, and some granola bars. Larry stocked a small cooler with water bottles and a couple of beers. When they arrived at the office, several other couples and two families were already gathered around two disreputable-looking stretch vans. One pulled a trailer stacked with eight canoes.

Mary Louise and a gangly college-aged boy came out of the office.

"Good afternoon, folks!" she boomed. "This is my nephew, Justin. We'll be taking you up to a little put-in north of here and on the other side of the river. Has everyone canoed before?" They all nodded and she continued.

"The float will take about two hours, depending on how often you stop. When you get back down here, you'll see warning signs along the river that you are approaching the take-out, and a big yellow sign right by the take-out. It's an easy landing—just pull your canoes up so others can get in and we'll take care of 'em."

While she spoke, Frannie scanned the rest of the group and realized with a shock that one of the other couples was Richard with a tall, dark-haired woman. He must know about Valerie; Larry had said that the sheriff's car was at Richard's camper when he and Mickey went up to make the reservations. Obviously, he wasn't devastated by her death. Maybe the woman was a relative or just a casual acquaintance but it still seemed odd. He didn't seem to recognize Frannie.

Mary Louise invited the group to board the vans. The Shoemakers and Ferraros climbed into the first one along with a younger couple and two boys, who looked to be about seven and ten. Richard and his companion got into the second van.

Mary Louise pulled herself up into the driver's seat and looked over at Mickey in the front passenger seat with a grin.

"You're a brave man."

Mickey was uncharacteristically silent for a moment, and then said, "You have a driver's license, right?"

Mary Louise let loose a guffaw. "Of course! Ever since Wednesday. That's why I'm having Justin pull the trailer."

Mickey grinned back, assuming—hoping—she was joking. Jane Ann leaned forward and said to Mary Louise, "Good one! He deserves that."

Soon they were on the road headed toward Burdensville, but crossed the river on an old bridge before they reached the town. Mary Louise seemed to have a couple of frustrated race car driver genes in her. Frannie could tell from Mickey's posture that he wasn't completely relaxed and smiled at his discomfort.

The caravan followed a gravel road north away from the river, climbing up into hills that framed the beautiful valley. The van rocked on the rough road, and the road noise made normal conversation difficult, although the two boys in back kept up a steady chatter about who was going to do what to whom once they were in the canoes. Mary Louise slowed the van and made a sharp turn down a dirt track. Frannie hoped that Justin, pulling the trailer, drove with a little more caution

Where they had occasionally passed farms and fields on the gravel, now overgrown, wild trees and shrubs encroached on the dirt road, threatening to return it to wilderness at any moment. After a winding descent back toward the river, Mary Louise stopped, put the van in park, and disembarked to open a large farm gate. She left it ajar and returned to the driver's seat, edging the vehicle forward along an even narrower track. Finally they reached an area that had been cleared out for a spacious turnaround.

Mary Louise braked the van, trumpeting "We're here! All out!"

They scrambled out, retrieving their coolers and other paraphernalia. Some of the younger members of the group helped Justin and Mary Louise lift the battered aluminum canoes off the rack and line them up near a path leading down toward a small creek.

Mary Louise explained the put-in. "This creek leads into the Burden about two hundred yards downstream. You might have to portage a little before you get to the river, but I think the water is high enough that if you get out, you should be able to float the canoes through. Just don't let go of that rope tied to the bow." Her laughter pealed merrily as she pointed to said rope on the nearest canoe. Justin stood by nodding his head, underlining her instructions.

They launched the families first, kids paddling crazily and switching sides with their paddles, scooping copious amounts of water into the canoes in the process.

Larry motioned to the other couples to go ahead. "At our ages, it won't be a fast launch," he said. Frannie noticed that Richard's manner toward his companion as he helped her into the canoe was probably not appropriate if she was a sister or friend. Richard gently put the paddle in her hands, speaking quiet, reassuring words. The woman appeared cautious and somewhat reluctant as she got in. Apparently, Valerie was not the only love of his life.

The last two canoes were dropped in for the Ferraros and the Shoemakers. Cement blocks had been embedded in the steep hillside to serve as steps. Jane Ann gingerly stepped into the bow of the first canoe while Justin and Mickey steadied it. Mickey got in the stern and picked up his paddle, pushing away from the bank.

Justin pulled the last canoe up to the little landing while Frannie and Larry threw their soft-sided cooler and visors in. Larry turned to ask Justin about the portage as Frannie placed her right foot in the center of the bow and leaned forward to grab the gunwales with each hand. Too late, she realized that the canoe did not sink in the water with her weight but instead sat on something solid. She pulled back as it tilted sideways toward the water. Her left foot slipped off the edge of a cement block, the canoe skidded out into the creek, and, arms flailing, she landed in the water up to her neck. The corner of one of the cement blocks gouged the right side of her back just above her waist.

She half sat, half lay in the shallow water as Justin and Larry both reached for her, firing questions the whole time.

"How did you do that?" her husband asked in disbelief.

"Are you okay?" Justin's voice was filled with concern, and behind him she could hear Mary Louise: "Oh, my!" For once there were no guffaws or peals of laughter.

With their help, she stood, sharp pain shooting through her side. At first, she couldn't seem to get her breath and ignored their questions. After a few moments she straightened up — well, mostly — and shook her head in response to whatever questions they were bombarding her with. She lifted the back of her shirt for Larry and Mary Louise to examine.

"No bleeding," Larry said. "You didn't break the skin. You're going to have a hell of a bruise, though, and be really sore."

Justin began apologizing. At his age, he probably thought he had just done in one of his grandmother's generation. "I'm really sorry — the keel must have been balanced on a rock underwater. I'm sorry...." He glanced helplessly at Mary Louise.

Frannie shook her head again. "I'm okay...my fault, too big a hurry..."

"We'll take you back to the campground and to the ER if you want," Mary Louise had regained her composure,

"No, really, I still want to go." She looked down the creek; Jane Ann and Mickey had already disappeared around a bend. There would be no way to tell them what had happened if they didn't go. "I'll be fine." She gave them all a weak smile and looked back at the canoe. Their little cooler, the lifejackets, and the visors floated in a couple inches of water.

"I'll dump it out," Justin said. Poor kid. He was ready to do anything to make amends.

"Don't worry about it," she insisted. "I've canoed for years, Justin. I know better than to step into a boat without checking first." He had pulled out the floating paraphernalia and lifted the side of the canoe to dump the water. He righted the canoe, relatively water free, and she carefully got into the bow seat while gritting her teeth at the stabs of pain. This time she made sure the craft was floating and that someone was steadying it. She asked Larry to prop the folded life jacket between her seat and the strut, giving her a sort of a back rest.

As they pushed off, Larry said, "Mickey and Jane Ann will think we fell in. Oh, wait, one of us did." He paused and then said, "That was mean, wasn't it? I'm sorry — sure you're going to be okay?"

She glanced back at him over her shoulder and smiled. "I deserve it. I should know better and, yes, I'll be okay. I'm just a little worried about that portage he mentioned."

"We'll find out soon enough." They glided along with minimum paddling through a green tunnel of overhanging trees. Frannie found that if she held herself quite erect and avoided twisting in either direction, it minimized the pain.

They rounded the bend in the creek and ahead lay a jut of sand and scraggly grasses covering most of the creek bed. The water coursed around to the right through a very rocky, narrow shoot. The stream moved fast, but was not deep enough to create a little riffle that they could easily ride through. So they would need to walk it through, using the rope. Jane Ann and Mickey stood at the downstream side of the spit, only about fifty feet away. Jane Ann held their canoe in place with the bow rope while they watched for Frannie and Larry to catch up.

Mickey hurried back to help pull their canoe up enough that they could get out. He held out a hand to Frannie.

"C'mon, old lady!" He was two months younger than Frannie and never passed up a chance to point it out.

This time she didn't argue with him. "Older than usual." She took his hand and let out a groan as he heaved her up out of the low seat.

"Frannie decided the usual boarding procedure was too dull and did a cartwheel to get into the canoe." Larry said, one foot out in the water to hold the canoe steady.

"Frannie, what happened?" Jane Ann called from her end of the spit.

"I'll leave the canoe to you guys. I can't do all of the work," Frannie told Larry and Mickey, and trudged through the scrubby grass toward Jane Ann. While Larry guided the canoe along the bank, Frannie filled Jane Ann in on her tumble. Jane Ann, a retired nurse, examined her bruise.

"Nasty scrape," she said. "Maybe you broke a rib."

Frannie looked at her in alarm. "I hope not! What do they do for that?"

"Nothing they can do. Painkillers. Can you take a deep breath?"

Frannie made the effort and the look of anguish on her face alarmed Jane Ann.

"I think when we get back, Larry should take you to the emergency room. Why did you even come on the float?"

"I don't think it's that bad," Frannie said. "Besides, there was no way to let you guys know what happened to us." She gave her sister-in-law a tentative smile.

"Oh, for heavens sakes! What if you had drowned? Would Larry have just thrown your body in the canoe so he could catch up and tell us what happened?"

Now Frannie gave her a full grin. "Probably."

Larry had gotten their canoe next to the Ferraros and held it parallel to the bank so that Frannie could get back in. After several Keystone Cops turns and a couple of gentle collisions, the two canoes were headed downstream. Frannie slowly leaned back on the makeshift backrest and tried to take a deep breath. Now the pain seemed worse. Fortunately, the current was such that she only needed to use her paddle occasionally to steer. And the pleasantly warm temperature made her wet clothes act as a cheap air conditioner.

The Ferraros pulled alongside and Jane Ann handed her an apple bar, one of their traditional canoeing treats, from a small plastic container.

"That should help," she said, and Frannie nodded happily, her mouth full.

Other than the pain, the float was very relaxing. The creek soon joined the Burden River and the waterway widened out, smooth as glass in some areas and gentle riffles in others. It headed generally southeast and would eventually join the Mississippi. They spotted a variety of birds along the banks, including a solitary white egret, and saw an occasional beaver, as well as a young fawn, drinking along the edge. She was so young, she didn't know to be frightened, and watched them as if perplexed by these odd human pastimes.

Frannie asked Larry for a water bottle out of the cooler, which he passed on the flat of his paddle across to Jane Ann, who handed it to Frannie so she wouldn't have to turn around. She moved as little as possible, hoping the beautiful surroundings would take her mind off what felt like a vice on her side. But, before long, the constriction prompted her to plead for a respite at the next sandbar.

"About time!" Mickey spouted. "No way I could ask for a break before you did."

Larry gently helped her out of the canoe. "It's hurting worse, isn't it?"

She nodded. "A little."

"A *lot*, I think. We'll go to the ER when we get back — no argument."

Jane Ann spread a disreputable old beach towel on the sand, the faded images of Donald Duck and family barely discernible. "Would it help to lay down?"

Frannie sighed. She hated giving in or being pampered but a short rest did sound good. "I think so."

"Maybe if you can get down on your hands and knees first...? I don't think we can lower you without hurting you worse," Jane Ann said. Frannie did as she was told and soon stared up at the amazingly blue sky above, the warm sand forming to and supporting her back an added bonus.

Larry opened a tub of party mix and passed it around. Frannie declined, thinking she didn't need to add choking to her ailments.

"Now, tell us how this happened," Mickey said. "Every gory detail." Larry obliged, too willingly, Frannie thought, complete with actions.

After about ten minutes, Frannie felt her back had relaxed enough that she requested help getting up. Larry assured her that they didn't want to hurry her, but on the other hand, the sooner they got back, the sooner they could have her injuries looked at. Once back on the river, they continued their steady progress back toward River Bend, waving at cyclists passing on the bike trail and residents in other riverside campgrounds.

CHAPTER EIGHT
SATURDAY MID-AFTERNOON

They reached a low jut of land before a high bluff and decided it might be the last possible bathroom stop for a while. Again, Larry eased the canoe in with as few jolts as possible. Jane Ann designated a clump of shrubbery as the Ladies' Loo. As Frannie waited in the canoe for the others to finish their business, she noticed a canoe downstream on the same side of the river, pulled up into some long grass. At first, there didn't appear to be anyone around—perhaps also using the facilities.

While she watched, a man and a woman seemed to pop out of the bluff near the canoe and then disappeared again. She realized with a bit of a jolt that it was Richard and his companion. In the trauma and pain of her fall, she had forgotten that he was on the float.

She pointed out the canoe to Larry as he launched. "That Richard guy and his Chick-of-the-Day are somewhere on that hillside but they show up and—pouf! —they're gone again. Are there caves around here?"

"I don't know about near the river. There's some back in the hills south of here."

Jane Ann was pushing off the bow of their boat. "That guy from the pie shop is on this float trip? Didn't the sheriff stop to tell him about the twins' death?"

"Yeah, we saw her car at his camper," Mickey said.

"I didn't recognize him. Are you sure it's the same guy? With another woman?" Jane Ann couldn't quite grasp this twist.

"It's definitely him—I saw him with Valerie last night." Frannie said. "I'm guessing that his feelings for Val weren't quite as deep as she thought."

"Maybe it's his sister or cousin," Larry said from the back of the canoe.

"If she's his sister, he treats her a lot more—shall we say, tenderly?—than you treat Jane Ann," she turned slightly to smirk at her husband, but instead winced as the pain seized her side.

"Doesn't pay to be a smartass," he said.

"I know," she grimaced. "My mother always told me that. We should check out that bluff—see where they went."

"No," said Larry.

The river made a big lazy loop, turning north, east and then back south. Nothing was required of Frannie, and it gave her a chance to think about the dead women and Richard. She wondered if the sheriff had actually talked to Richard and if so, what she had found out. Maybe the sheriff hadn't found him yet; he could have been out on his bike. She didn't want to think that he was that much of a scumbag to lead two women on at once. She was enough of a romantic to want Val's hopes had some foundation, even though those hopes had evaporated at the power plant.

The loop ended and the river turned east. As they rounded the bend, the ominous hulk of the power plant —now even more so with its recent history—came into view on the right bank. A small sand bar jutted out at the base.

"Can we stop?" Frannie asked.

"Because you're hurting or because you're nosey?" Larry kept paddling at a steady rate.

"Well…"

"*We* are heading to the ER as soon as we get off this river. *If* the doctor says you haven't broken anything and *if* they also say you are allowed *mild* activity, we will visit the Power Plant *later*, okay?" The paddle chopped through the water to emphasize each condition he gave her.

"Geesh. What a grouch," said Jane Ann, coming up on their left side.

Mickey agreed. "She just wants to do a little investigating."

"Exactly what I'm worried about," Larry answered. "With any luck at all, they'll keep her in the hospital for six days."

"But we're only here for *five* days," Frannie protested.

Larry grinned. "I'll wait for you."

As they passed the gray, crumbling relic, Frannie examined it thoughtfully. What could possibly have led to the deaths of two women in their prime? The night before, they talked enthusiastically about their careers and their travels—as the saying goes, not a care in the world. Now they were both gone. It didn't seem like they could be a threat to anyone.

They reached the western edge of the campground, and back in the trees she spotted the derelict camper the men had seen the night before. A young man, about eighteen or nineteen, carried wood from a stack behind the camper to a fire pit in front. Compared to the man she had seen in the pickup the night before, this guy looked pretty clean cut. Almost too clean cut—kind of a skinhead look. When he glanced up, his look was stoic and certainly not friendly. Maybe the twins *had* put themselves in danger with their cameras. He watched them pass and then turned back to his task.

They followed another large loop around the campground; hence the name River Bend. At the end of the loop they found a wide, gentle takeout, and waiting at the top of the slope, Mary Louise Larson and her golf cart.

"Yoohoo!" she called, beaming with relief. "You made it—I've been worried!"

Larry tried to gently coax the canoe up to the slope, but even a slight bump caused sharp jabs in Frannie's side. Mary Louise's expression changed from outright joy to concern as she saw Frannie's face.

"You *are* hurting! Time to get you looked at!" She sidestepped down the slope to the canoe, steadied the bow, and reached out a hand to Frannie to help her out. It wasn't a pretty dismount.

"I'll give you a ride in the cart to your site," Mary Louise continued, and then looked back at Larry. "You can take her to the ER right away, can't you?"

Larry grinned. "That's the plan. Besides, I wouldn't dare say no to you, Mary Louise."

"Well, look at her! I should have insisted on bringing her back with us."

Frannie thought she'd better step in and defend her husband before Mary Louise really took him on. "Thanks for your concern, but it really hasn't been that bad — most of the time. Don't blame Larry; he can't do anything with me when I've made up my mind. I will accept the offer of the ride, though."

Mary Louise tried to gently hustle her up the slope and into the cart. While the others hauled the canoes and paddles to the top of the little hill, Mary Louise chatted about who had already arrived and who hadn't. Frannie noticed that Richard and his companion were among the yet-to-arrive.

Frannie appreciated not having to walk from the takeout to the campsite, but the golf cart was not exactly a smooth ride. Mary Louise kept up a constant commentary on previous injuries she and her children had suffered, who provided the best medical care in the area, and what the extent of Frannie's injuries might be. At least Frannie didn't feel obliged to reply at any length because speaking was becoming more of an effort.

When they arrived at the campsite, Ben and Nancy were back from the high ropes course and helped her to one of the reclining lawn chairs. By the time Mary Louise had given them a detailed account of the accident, Larry, Mickey and Jane Ann were rounding the corner. Larry went in the camper to get his keys and billfold. Using a small folding step-stool, the hand holds inside the truck, and several hands, the others helped Frannie into the passenger side of the truck.

The nearest emergency clinic was small and enjoying a fairly quiet afternoon. "The rush will come this evening, with sunburns and injuries that people don't think are that bad until they try to go to sleep," the nurse told the Shoemakers.

After a short wait and a recap of her medical history, Frannie was subjected to x-rays and some poking and prodding that didn't make the injury feel any better. Another wait, and a young physician's assistant, Dr. Havek, told her that the x-rays did not show any fractures, "although there could be one so small that it isn't showing up." Great.

He recommended an over-the-counter pain reliever and rest.

"How long?"

"How long what?"

"How long do I have to rest? Just today?"

The young man looked at her suspiciously. "What did you have in mind?"

"Can I go hiking? Or biking?"

"What kind of hiking? Up and down cliffs?"

"No." Frannie let out a snort. "I don't do that when I'm well. Just on the bike path."

Larry, standing to the side of the examining table, rolled his eyes. Dr. Havek put down his clipboard, leaned against the counter, and folded his arms.

"You can walk *slowly*, but don't do anything that could bring another fall. You are going to be very sore for weeks — maybe months."

"Months?!?"

"Told you so," Larry muttered.

"This kind of injury doesn't heal fast, and especially in older people," Dr. Havek said.

"You don't have to be mean about it," Frannie said. "I'm not *that* old."

"Just giving you the facts. Do you have any other questions?" So much for bedside manner.

"No."

"Well, take care, Mrs. Shoemaker. I hope the rest of your trip is less eventful." He nodded at them both, picked up his clipboard, and left.

"I guess that means we're done," Larry said, helping her off the examining table.

They checked out, and with some effort and Larry's aid, Frannie managed to climb back up into the truck. When they returned to the campground, she reluctantly tolerated a great deal of fussing, but was finally ensconced in her recliner, book and iced tea at hand, a couple of painkillers down her gullet, and an almost flat pillow behind her back for a little support. She realized it was the first time, other than a few minutes stretched out on a sandbar, that she could completely relax since her fall.

Nancy sat down beside her, concern showing in her face.

Frannie grimaced a little. "I thought I was taking the safe route. How were the high ropes?"

"Oh, awesome! Ben and I went through two of them. They're about thirty-five feet above the ground—" she smiled as Frannie grimaced a lot. "Really, it's not bad. You have safety lines on the whole time..."

Frannie was shaking her head. "I'm glad you had fun, Nancy, but no way. I don't even like to get on stepladders."

Rob and Donna returned and Donna was torn between sympathy and a little pique at having been shoved out of first place in the injury department. But after plying Frannie with what seemed like endless questions, she settled in a chair beside Frannie, sharing recipes that caught her eye in a magazine.

The painkillers, exhaustion, and the lazy afternoon sun took their toll and soon Frannie nodded off, despite Donna's best efforts.

But not for long. Mary Louise Larson's booming voice jarred her awake in time to hear Mary Louise say, "Oh, my, were you sleeping? Don't let me bother you. I just wanted to see how you are doing and what the doctor said. I'll check with your husband—pay no attention to me and go back to sleep." Right.

But she did let Larry do the play-by-play from the clinic while she tried to keep a vacant smile on her face, still not quite awake. Finally Mary Louise patted her hand, saying, "I'm so glad nothing's broken—although sometimes a bruise can be worse. I brought some ice cream bars down because I think ice cream is good for any injury, don't you?" She kept her laugh at a low rumble in deference to Frannie's fragile condition.

Frannie agreed and thanked her. Mary Louise hurried back to her golf cart, promising to check on them later. As the cart moved out of the way, Frannie noticed that the sheriff's car was back at the twins' trailer and crime scene tape had been strung around the campsite.

Frannie had dozed off again when the sheriff walked over. "Mrs. Shoemaker?"

Frannie sat up, winced and looked around, momentarily confused. The rest of the group had apparently gone in to begin supper preparations.

"Call me Frannie, please."

"Is something wrong? You look uncomfortable." Frannie gave her a much briefer and less dramatic rendering than Larry would have.

"Wow. That's a bummer. Quite a day you've had." She sat down in a vacant lawn chair.

"Not one I'd care to repeat. Have you found out any more about how those women died?"

Sheriff Sorensen shook her head. "Haven't gotten the ME's report yet. Remember, he's got two to do."

"Can I ask you something?" Frannie said.

"You can ask. I may or may not answer," Mary Sorensen smiled.

"Did you talk to that guy Richard? Does he know about the deaths?"

"I can't tell you what he said."

"But you did talk to him? That's all I want to know."
Well, not really, but it was a start.

"Yes, I did talk to him," Sorensen conceded.

"Well, did he—?" Frannie began, but stopped when she saw the sheriff shaking her head. She explained. "He was on the same float trip this afternoon that we were on. With another woman. He didn't seem very broken up, so if you had already given him the news, I'm thinking what Valerie told me must have been pretty one-sided."

"Maybe."

Frannie sighed, as Cuba nosed up to her side, sensing she needed consoling. "You really *aren't* going to tell me anything."

"No. But you can tell me anything else *you've* thought of."

Frannie shrugged. "I haven't thought of anything else. I'm kind of suspicious of those guys in the old trailer. We came by there this afternoon and it's a creepy looking place. The camera bag didn't ever turn up?"

"No, it didn't."

"Makes me wonder what kind of pictures they took of those guys. Could have been something incriminating."

"Maybe," Sorensen said again, getting up. "I do have one other question for you. Have you seen anyone else around that trailer since you got here yesterday?"

Frannie thought a moment. "No. Only the twins last night and this morning."

"Okay, thanks. Take care of yourself." And she was back in her car.

Frannie leaned back in her chair. Her little nap seemed to have helped; she was feeling better. She swung her legs off the chair and started to ease herself up. A screen door squeaked, as Jane Ann came out of their motorhome, carrying a tray.

"What did the sheriff want?"

"To know if we'd seen anything we haven't told her about."

"I can't think of anything. Where are you going?"

"To the bathroom."

"Maybe you should just use the one in the trailer," Jane Ann said.

"Thanks for your concern. I know you mean well, but I really am just sore and walking doesn't hurt. The doctor basically said no mountain climbing. Besides the shower house is better equipped for us handicapped folks than the trailer is." Frannie smiled.

Jane Ann wasn't giving up. "Do you want me to go along?"

"No, I'll be fine." She headed to the road, holding herself carefully so she didn't wince. Actually, if she didn't twist or turn, it felt rather good to move a little. As the road turned, she looked back (carefully) and saw Jane Ann still watching her. She gave a little wave, almost tripped because she wasn't looking where she was going, and refocused on staying upright.

The campground was full this weekend and people in almost every campsite were busy with supper preparations. Kids on bikes, scooters and skateboards raced by her in a never-ending chase, and dogs reacted to her passing with raucous barks, yips, growls and just bored stares.

As she left the bathroom, she glanced over at Richard's site and noticed he was sitting by his camper in a lawn chair. She stepped off the road, watching for uneven ground.

"Excuse me?"

He turned in the chair, closing his magazine, and looked at her, raising his eyebrows. He still showed no sign of recognizing her.

"Yes?"

She plunged ahead. Larry would kill her. "I'm sorry to bother you but just wanted to express my condolences. I understand you knew the twins…?"

"Well, I wouldn't say *knew* them, not well anyway—I had met one of them on a cruise several years ago. Not sure which one—Val, I think."

Even though she had suspected him of being a womanizer after seeing him on the float that afternoon, she was still taken aback at his detachment. He also didn't remember her walking with Val the evening before. Obviously she was too old to warrant his attention.

But she said, "Oh, I see. I misunderstood."

He gave a wry smile. "Apparently the sheriff did also. She stopped earlier; I guess someone told her I was in a romantic relationship with one of the women. But we were only casual acquaintances." He examined her rather accusingly.

Frannie nodded, wondering at the same time if she could find a casual acquaintance to buy her a necklace like Val's.

"Apparently you knew them?"

Frannie shrugged. "Not really. They were camped across the road from us and we visited with them last night a little bit." She decided not to mention that they had also found the bodies. "I need to go. Sorry to bother you."

He said, "No problem," and went back to his magazine before she had even gotten turned around for her careful trek back to the road.

By the time she returned to the campsite, supper preparations were in full swing. She couldn't even remember what they had planned to have until she saw Larry removing salmon filets from a plastic bag of marinade and carefully arranging them in the fish baskets.

He looked up when she approached the table, frowning.

CHAPTER NINE

SATURDAY EVENING

"I know, I know, I was out without permission," Frannie said.

"You should at least let someone go along, in case you pass out or something."

She sighed and let herself down carefully on the picnic table bench to watch his preparations. Donna sat down rather heavily beside her, causing the bench to bounce. Frannie tried not to flinch.

"How are you feeling?" Donna's voice was full of concern.

"Quite a bit better with some aspirin and a little nap."

"We've got a great supper almost ready. Salmon, you know, and I made some of those rolls of mine that you love. Jane Ann's working on a salad and Nancy has those bacon and cheese potatoes in the slow cooker."

"Sounds fantastic. Can I do anything? Set the table?" Frannie smiled. She wasn't used to Donna being so gracious, although as Frannie had come to know her better on an earlier trip, she now found her less abrasive than she used to. Or, at least Frannie was more willing to overlook a lot of Donna's outrageous behavior.

Donna got up, bouncing the bench again. "No—sit tight. Or whatever makes you comfortable." She smiled sympathetically. "We have it covered. Do you want your chair over here?"

This might be the only time ever that Donna waited on her, instead of the other way around. "Sure."

Donna dragged the recliner over, retrieved the pillow from where she had dropped it in the dust, pounded it off, and moved a little table next to the chair.

"Can I get you more iced tea? Or are you ready for some wine?"

"Tea would be great," Frannie answered. "I'd better wait on the wine." She got herself arranged in the chair again, and watched Larry baste the filets on the grill. Jane Ann set a bowl of coleslaw on the table and pulled a lawn chair up beside Frannie.

"So what did the sheriff have to say? Did she tell you anything?"

Frannie shook her head, trying to ignore Larry's scrutiny. He believed she was meddling in police business again. Not that she had ever *really* meddled— she just had ideas that sometimes turned out to be correct.

"The ME hasn't finished the autopsies yet. Other than that, her lips were sealed."

"Unlike some people I could name," Larry said.

"You *are* a grouch today," Jane Ann told her brother. "Frannie can hardly get in much trouble—she can barely move."

"I wish I believed that," he mumbled.

Mickey showed up with a tray of more salmon. "Larry's always a grouch. That's nothing new." Before it could turn into one of their regular sparring matches, Nancy appeared with a tablecloth and tray of citrus-hued plastic dishes and silverware.

"Okay, guys, this stuff has to go somewhere else while I set the table." She started moving the trays and bowls to the bench and small tables. Mickey jumped up to help her.

"Wow. Check it out. We are all underdressed." Donna stood, hands on her ample hips, staring out at the main road. Frannie followed her gaze. A tall woman, not heavy but thick through the middle, wobbled along on spike heels and a strapless, very fitted, very short rose-colored dress. Her hair was piled high in an elaborate hairstyle difficult to fully appreciate from this distance but certainly requiring more than the wake and shake that Frannie practiced.

Mickey looked up from the grill. "Whoa! Jane Ann, you could take a page from her book!"

Frannie let out such a snort that she had to hold her side. "Mickey, you idiot! You're married to Grace Kelly and are lusting after Miss Trailer Trash of 1982?"

"Careful, missy—you're currently living in a trailer yourself, remember?" Larry said.

Jane Ann laid her hand on Frannie's arm. "Thanks, Frannie, but remember he had brain damage after tripping on his tongue years ago."

"Explains a lot," Frannie nodded.

The woman continued down the road toward the far end of the campground. They were all so engrossed in watching her halting progress that Mary Louise's voice, startling in any circumstances, made them all jump.

"I see you've noticed our budding country star!" She walked over from where she had parked her golf cart at the next campsite.

"Country star?" Nancy asked doubtfully.

"Jonie's been on the 'verge of a breakthrough' for about twenty years. Every couple of years, she scrapes together enough cash for a trip to Nashville, knocks on doors, and comes back home to wait for calls." Mary Louise pushed some stray hair back behind her barrettes. "Meantime, she sings for tips at a county line tavern near here. And I don't think she's above the poverty level, if you get my meaning." She paused a minute. "She stands to inherit a lot of money someday from her uncle but he's one of those ornery old coots who might live to 125 just to spite people."

"She walks out here? In *those* shoes?" Donna couldn't believe anyone walking more than two or three blocks, and had forgotten her own foot troubles the day before from her 'cute' shoes.

"Naw, she hitches rides and they drop her at the campground entrance. I think she's interested in Mel Dubrak in that old camper you saw yesterday. At least that's where she goes."

"You don't have to let her come through here, do you?" Larry asked.

Mary Louise let out a big breath. "No, I don't. But I don't mind. We've never seen any reason to stop them coming through here."

"I don't want to cast unfounded accusations, Mary Louise, but you'd better be a little careful in that area," Larry said.

Mickey called, "Plate!" as if they weren't all within ten feet of him. Nancy held out a platter and he opened each filet basket, gently coaxing the fragrant contents on to the serving plate. She walked around to Larry and he did the same.

"Man, you guys do know how to rough it," Mary Louise said, admiring the array of bowls and baskets on the table. "I'll get out of here and let you enjoy it." They said their goodbyes as they took their places at the table. Frannie declined offers to bring her a plate and took a spot on the end of the bench, easier to get into.

She gazed around at her friends, laughing and juggling plates and bowls, and the beautiful evening and thought of all the tragedy and pain of the day. Life is weird. The twins were very casual acquaintances, but that brief encounter was enough to snag a little part of her soul. She wondered if the sheriff had found any family to contact. To her knowledge, the only person whom she thought had a close connection, Richard, claimed it wasn't that close. Mickey pulled her out of her reverie asking if she had a head injury. She responded maturely by sticking out her tongue and focused on the conversation.

After the meal and kitchen chores were done, the whole group decided on a stroll around the campground. The dogs were leashed up and Frannie declined an offer to be pulled in the collapsible wagon that they used to move firewood. When they reached the main campground road, they decided to head west, hoping to see the beaver at work again in the river.

Along the way, they met Jonie, the rising country star, hobbling along toward them, returning from the trailer.

"Hey!" she called out as she approached. "Nahce nahght!" Her attempted Tennessee twang would not have gotten her a part in a local high school play, even in a very small school.

"Sure is," Larry replied, tugging back on Cuba's leash. At her age, she was no threat to anyone but still big enough to frighten people not fond of dogs.

"Any of you folks headed inta town later?"

"Sorry, I don't think so," Mickey said, sounding sincere enough to get a tweak on his arm from his wife.

"Awright—thanks anyway. Say, gonna be around a few days? You oughta come see my show—I'm a singer," she actually batted her eyelashes. "And I perform almost every night up at Farrell's on the county line. Name's Jonie Rump, but my stage name's Jonie Helene." Her accent slipped the more she talked.

"Thanks, we'll keep that in mind," Frannie said. She ignored the look from Jane Ann.

Jonie gave them a coquettish little wave and sashayed by. When she was out of earshot, Jane Ann mumbled to Frannie, "Rump? Are you kidding me?"

Frannie shrugged in innocence. "I didn't say a word."

"Jonie Boob is more like it."

Frannie giggled. They were trailing behind the others, and Larry turned around to check on her.

"Are you getting too tired? We can go back."

"No. I'm fine. I haven't done anything all day."

"Just found a couple of bodies and made a spectacular one-point landing. Probably would have only scored about a six but spectacular anyway."

Actually, she had been thinking about turning around soon but now decided to stick with the group.

"Technically, Donna found the bodies."

"Whatever."

When they got to the river, they saw no sign of the beavers. The setting sun filtered through the trees but the river was already dark in most places. The derelict trailer could only be glimpsed through the trees, small, angry, and threatening. Frannie saw no sign of life around it. They headed back to the campsite and settled into their favorite night time activity, sitting around the fire.

"What's for breakfast?" Mickey said. A vigorous discussion ensued. Frannie didn't know from experience about armies, but there was no doubt in her mind that campers definitely traveled on their stomachs. Soon she excused herself, received several sympathetic looks and went in to bed.

She woke in the night, tried to turn over and was punished for her efforts with a stab in her side. After trying several positions, she gave up and got out of bed to take another aspirin. She finished the glass of water, opened the camper door, and peered outside. The entire campground was dark and quiet. A few coals still glowed in the fire pit and the night was so filled with stars that there seemed no room for any more.

She went out and sat on the steps, wrapping her arms around herself, and took breaths as deep as she could manage of the cool night air. What a beautiful night. The breeze was light and made occasional rustling sounds in the trees and shrubs. A few scratching and scrambling sounds attested to the presence of wild creatures. No doubt the raccoons were checking out opportunities at every campsite. There were no lights, but she could make out the light-colored shape of Ferraros' motor home, the darker shapes of trees towering above it, and in the distance, a faint whitish smudge against the sky marking the top of the limestone bluffs across the river.

She again puzzled over the strange relationship between the twins and Richard, and caught the reflection of a small light against the Nowaks' trailer across the road. It must be coming from the vicinity of the twins' trailer, out of Frannie's line of sight. Someone was over there; not likely the authorities at this hour, and there was no sign of a vehicle. A cold lump of fear gathered in the pit of her stomach and she held her breath. She thought she could hear sounds from that direction, but not that different from what she had earlier interpreted as raccoons.

She carefully stood on the steps and as quietly as she could, turned around and opened the camper door. She mounted the steps and eased in the door. It didn't take much to cause the trailer to rock and roll.

She should be able to see the twins' trailer from the window over the couch, so she edged over to the couch, and kneeling on it, parted two of the slats on the blinds and peered out.

The light came from inside the trailer, bouncing from window to window. Where had she laid her phone the night before? Sometimes she put it on the table or the end counter; sometimes in a jacket pocket.

She was pretty sure that last night she had put it on the table. Checking to make sure the light was still inside the trailer across the road, she crept the few steps from the couch to the table, making sure not to fall over the dog. A little glow from a night light made the black rectangle stand out on the light colored table top. When she turned it on, she noticed it was after 3:00. She dialed 911 and quietly explained the situation to the dispatcher, mentioning Mary Sorenson, and that the trailer belonged to the dead women. As she shut off the phone, she started at a rustling noise and looked around to see the shape of her husband in the bedroom doorway.

"What's going on?" The bear just emerging from hibernation.

"Someone is in the twins' trailer," Frannie said.

"Maybe the sheriff," Larry said, bending over to squint through the blinds.

"At this hour?"

"Not the sheriff," he amended. "He's leaving and it's definitely not Mary Sorenson."

Frannie kneeled beside him on the couch to get another look. A figure taller than Mary ducked under the crime scene tape and headed to the wooded slope at the back of the campground.

"Maybe we should..."

"No," Larry said firmly. "We shouldn't. He may be armed, he has a head start and certainly is younger than we are. Also, he may not be alone."

Frannie hadn't thought of that. She continued to watch the trailer for an accomplice and saw no sign of anyone else. But she supposed there could be someone waiting in the woods. She sighed and stood up, avoiding sudden twists.

"I wonder what they would be looking for? Could you tell if he was carrying anything?"

"Too dark." Larry stuck his perpetual travel mug of coffee in the microwave to reheat.

Frannie unsnapped the lid of a plastic container on the counter. "Cookie?" she asked, taking one and holding out the container to Larry. He took two.

"We might as well get comfortable." He dropped in his recliner, snapping it back. Frannie cringed at the sound but realized the intruder was nowhere close by now. She poured herself a glass of milk by the light from the refrigerator, and sat down to wait. It was like waiting out a power outage or a tornado warning in their basement at home. Nothing to do but think.

Larry looked at her. "How did you know there was something going on?"

"I woke up and couldn't get comfortable. So I took some aspirin and went out to sit on the steps a minute. It was so peaceful and beautiful."

Larry sat up. "Frannie, did you go over there?"

"No, I did not. I saw the light and came in immediately and looked out the window. Since the sheriff's car wasn't there and it was so late, I called 911."

She half expected a pat on the back for her good sense —not always so evident—but the closest Larry could manage was a grudging, "Good."

They sat in silence a little longer until they saw headlights coming up the camp road. Larry went to the kitchen window.

"It's the sheriff. You stay here."

She didn't argue, but adjusted the nearest blinds so that she could see out without moving.

Larry and the sheriff were silhouetted against the car headlights. Sorenson nodded at Larry's explanation and then walked to the trailer door, hand on her gun. Frannie couldn't see the actual door and waited, drumming her fingers on the dinette table. Finally, the sheriff came back around the corner, and as she and Larry stood talking, while he pointed in the direction they had seen the intruder go, two more cars pulled up. Several officers joined them, one with a large dog on a leash.

Flashlights bounced along the ground as the officers headed toward the slope and Larry returned to their camper.

"Obviously, no one was in there," Frannie said to him. "Did she find anything else?"

"Oh, yes, someone was definitely looking for something. She said drawers were pulled out—quite a mess."

"Seems to me that indicates that the twins' deaths were not just random. There are more layers to this than it appears."

"Frannie," Larry hesitated, leaned against the counter and folded his arms. "No offense, honey, but the police— or in this case, the sheriff and deputies—aren't idiots. They've done this before, and they will do it again. They were sure this wasn't random by yesterday afternoon."

"Oh." Frannie sat looking at her hands feeling foolish. Larry was right, she was trying to interfere and didn't know what she was doing. She was suddenly exhausted, and even though she was dying to know if the deputies caught anyone, she recognized her limits.

"I think I'll go back to bed," she said, standing with some effort.

"Good idea. I'm not trying to belittle the help you've given them…"

She waved him off. "I know. You're right. But maybe I can sleep now—I am so tired."

And she did. Laying flat on her back, she felt relief from the tension and pain and immediately dropped off.

CHAPTER TEN

SUNDAY MORNING

The next morning, Frannie awoke to the patter of rain on the camper roof. Odd, there hadn't been a cloud in the sky a few hours before. She smiled to herself. Not that odd, really; she'd lived in the Midwest her whole life and shouldn't be surprised by sudden turns in the weather. So much for Mickey's forecast.

She eased out of bed so as not to disturb Larry, and slipped on a hooded sweatshirt and slippers. After plugging in the coffee pot they had readied the night before, she raised the blinds and looked out. Not a heavy rain, and the sky appeared lighter off in the West. But the firewood would be wet; maybe it was a good day for an easy breakfast. She got a container of veggie pancakes out of the freezer.

Sitting in Larry's recliner, waiting for the coffee, her thoughts were drifting when her phone chirped for a text message. It was from Jane Ann: MYBE BRFST INSIDE THIS MORN? Obviously, great minds do run along the same track. Frannie replied, GOING TO WRM UP VGGI PANCAKES. Ten seconds later, an answer: B RITE THERE.

Frannie smiled. NOT YET. LARRY'S STILL IN BED. The response: FIGURES. K.

By the time Larry got up, and the group shared a throw-together breakfast of the pancakes, fruit, and leftover rolls from Donna's purchase on Friday, the sky had cleared and the grass glistened with the rain drops. Everyone trooped outside and wiped down tables and chairs while making plans for the day's ride from Wheat Valley.

Jane Ann straightened from wiping the picnic table bench. "Frannie, what about you?"

"Well, the doctor didn't say I couldn't, but this morning I'm thinking I will pass."

"I'll stay here, too," Larry said.

"Don't be silly. I've got plenty to read and I'm sure Mary Louise will be by to check on me."

"I know you," Larry insisted. "You have something planned. You need to stay out of this investigation."

She shook her head and held up three fingers. "Scout's honor. I will be in that recliner except for trips to the bathroom. I don't feel that bad—I just don't want to take any chances." And she meant it.

Larry put up more objections and Frannie parried them all. Finally, she said, "When you get back, you can make it up to me with a trip to the pie shop." He gave up.

In another hour the bikes were loaded and they were ready for departure. Larry offered again to stay with her, as did Jane Ann. As further proof of her intentions, she brought three paperbacks and her ereader out of the camper, plus a bag with a gaudy purple scarf she was knitting for her granddaughter, Sabet. Larry brought the old percolator out to the utility table and plugged it in the exterior outlet and also handed her cell phone to her.

Mickey said, "I think we have an old port-a-potty in the back of a storage compartment, if you need it."

"Ewwww," said Frannie. "I believe I'm well enough to go in and use the private facilities."

After Donna made two trips back into her camper, first for sunglasses and then a water bottle, they launched. Frannie sat for a while, totally relaxed, drinking in the pleasant morning. Since it was Sunday, several people were starting to pack up and get ready to head home. School was still in session and, oh yeah, some people had to work.

She picked up a John Sanford mystery that she was almost finished with and began reading. Cuba curled up on the ground beside her with a deep sigh. Boring mistress. Frannie was at an exciting spot in the book but the laziness of the morning and the lack of sleep the night before conspired against her and soon she dozed off. She had been asleep a half hour or more when the sound of a car woke her.

Sheriff Mary Sorenson walked toward her chair, looking as crisp and efficient as usual.

"Good morning!"

"A beautiful one," Frannie agreed.

Sorenson looked around at the campsites. "Did they all abandon you?"

Frannie nodded. "We had been planning to do the segment of trail from Wheat Valley today. I didn't want to take a chance on another fall, and I fought off all attempts made for anybody to stay here and *hover.*"

"Well, it looks like you have plenty to keep you occupied," Mary nodded at the stack of books. "I wanted to ask you about last night."

"I take it you didn't catch anyone?"

"No, but we could see where he—or she—headed into the woods. How did you happen to notice someone was in there?"

Frannie repeated her account of waking up and going outside.

"And you only saw one person leave the trailer?"

"Yes."

"How long do you think they were in there?"

Frannie shrugged. "It must have been at least fifteen minutes from when I noticed the light until we saw them leave. But I don't know how long the person had already been in there when I noticed the light. I don't think I looked over that way when I first came out. Could you tell what they were looking for?"

"No, I keep thinking cameras and incriminating pictures, since that was their occupation."

"And since at least one camera bag is missing, that seems likely," Frannie agreed. "We know they took some pictures of that derelict trailer—they told us that Friday night. How did they die, do you know yet?"

"Preliminary results show that the one you think is Virginia died from hitting her head on the machinery, but she appears to have a blow on the other side of her head.

Someone hit her with something and knocked her into the machinery."

"And Valerie?" Frannie asked.

"She was strangled," Sorenson replied.

"Isn't that odd? Two deaths so close together by different means?"

"It certainly isn't common but not unheard of. "

"I mean, Virginia—that sounds like someone striking out in anger—maybe even an accident; but strangling? That's very deliberate—and personal."

"Usually. This whole case is very odd. And we can't find any relatives. They worked free-lance so even the people they worked for didn't know them very well. At least you won't have to worry about intruders tonight. We'll be pulling that trailer out of here today. We didn't get to it yesterday because with the primary crime scene so exposed to the elements, we wanted to focus on that first."

"Has the media picked up on this yet? We don't watch much TV when we're camping."

"Last night they broke the story. I'm sure they'll be snooping around here today—that's another reason to get this trailer moved. If they do come by, it would be better if you didn't answer questions. Especially don't tell anyone about the incident last night. The intruder may think that no one even knows he was there." Sorenson stood. "Don't hesitate to call if you think of something else from last night."

Frannie agreed and watched her drive away. She appreciated that Mary Sorenson seemed to value her opinion and observations without getting too chummy. Larry thought Frannie interfered too much—tried to play detective, and she had gotten in some dangerous scrapes before, but she had no intention of doing that this time.

She picked up her book and quickly finished the last twenty pages. During the next hour, she took a little walk to the main road, knitted on the scarf for a while, and started another book. She was in the trailer slicing up an apple when a TV van arrived.

She returned to her chair and watched with interest while a short, trim brunette directed another young woman with a camera around the site of the small trailer. The brunette picked the spot festooned with the most crime scene tape and brandished her mike, her wrinkle-free face trying to convey the weight of the world's problems as she worked to convince the camera of her authority.

Frannie couldn't hear what the brunette was saying, but amused herself by supplying the commentary. *Authorities aren't saying*...no, there would be clever references to the unique victims...*Twins from the Twin Cities*...except Minnesotans just said 'the Cities'...*Double jeopardy found these sisters in an old power plant*...ooh, bad...*These sisters were victims of 'photo'copy murders*...

"Ma'am?" The brunette approached her chair and Frannie quickly wiped the little smirk off her face.

"Yes?"

"Ma'am, did you know the two women staying in that trailer?"

"Not really," Frannie said. Larry would be so proud.

"I'm sure you know they were found murdered yesterday?" There was a slight hopeful note in her voice that Frannie had not heard the news and would display video-worthy shock. Like they could have a yellow tape-wrapped camper across from them and not notice.

"Yes, we heard that. Absolutely awful."

"Do you think...?" She pulled the mike back up into position when she was distracted by a procession of vehicles down the narrow road. A deputy's car led, with a pickup behind and a local police car bringing up the rear. The camera person ran around to the driver's side of the van and jumped in to move it.

"Oh! I'd better...," said the brunette and rushed off to join her companion. Frannie hoped she completed more of her sentences while on the air.

They moved the TV van farther down the road and the other vehicles pulled in around the little German trailer, with the pickup backing into position to hitch it up. Frannie watched the process with interest and the reporter's attempts to get comments from the deputy with amusement. The pickup driver knew what he was doing and made all the necessary connections and disconnections to make the trailer road-ready. Soon the TV van left, and not long after, the pickup pulled the trailer out, followed by the patrol cars.

Frannie got up and moved her chair to follow the shade. She was just getting resettled when she heard the puttering of a golf cart. And Larry was worried about her being alone.

Mary Louise, today in a lime green shimmering top, hefted a plastic container out of the back.

"Hallo!" she called as she walked up. "I brought us some lunch to share. I promised your husband I would check on you."

"Figures," Frannie said. "He's convinced that on my own, I will only get into trouble."

Mary Louise looked at her sideways, while she removed two large, plastic wrapped plates from the container. "I made us some coleslaw and crab salad pitas. Does he have reason to think you would get into trouble?"

"Wellll," Frannie said, and, while Mary Louise unwrapped the plates and set out flatware and napkins, she recounted two previous camping trips when they had become involved in a murder and a kidnapping case.

"Wow," said Mary Louise as she sat down heavily at the table. "I guess I should have done background checks before I rented you guys sites." She grinned.

Frannie joined her at the table.

"But it was pretty scary both times," Frannie confessed. "And there's nothing I can do here—nobody knows anything about them and I'm pretty crippled up."

Mary Louise nodded, her mouth full. After she swallowed, she said, "Well, just between us, what do you *think* happened?"

Frannie thought about it a moment, chewing on her own delicious sandwich. "It's hard to guess. I can't imagine what they could have done to make someone lash out at them like that." She debated with herself what information she could share without violating the sheriff's instructions.

"Well," Mary Louise said, "the sheriff said it appears that they didn't go to the power plant together. She asked us if we had seen the pickup leave. My husband, Jim, was working outside at the time and said there was only one of them in the truck."

Frannie nodded. "That's what I saw too. We thought maybe one of them wanted to hike and the other didn't so they agreed to meet there."

"Maybe. But why were they even there? They asked me the day before about the wildlife sanctuary—said they planned to go there to take some pictures."

"These sandwiches are excellent, Mary Louise. Thanks for bringing them. I suppose they may have wanted to get some photos around the power house or from the windows…it is a puzzle."

"That power plant is so spooky. You know there is a tunnel that connects it to a bend upriver?"

"You're kidding. What for?"

"I guess it diverted the water and created more fall to help generate the power. There's lots of local legends about how it was dug by hand by immigrant miners, and later, after the plant was shut down, supposedly bootleg liquor from Canada was hidden there."

"Huh. We have a lot of similar stories in Eastern Iowa about the rum runners—usually involving gangsters out of Chicago."

"I don't know how much is true. Jim grew up around here and always heard a lot of stories. He could tell you more about it."

"I'd *love* to hear more about it," Frannie said. "I used to be a history teacher in real life. Tell me, do you remember the last name of that guy Richard in the blue pickup across from your office?"

Mary Louise raised her eyebrows. "Oh, yes, it's Ellis-Reynolds. La-de-da. Pretty fancy for a guy with a pickup and a topper, dontcha think? What's the deal with him, anyway? The sheriff asked, too, and went to talk to him."

Frannie filled her in on Valerie Peete's supposed romance with Richard.

"Huh. He seemed pretty chummy with the dark-haired chick on the float yesterday." Mary Louise crumpled up the plastic wrap and stacked Frannie's plate on her own.

"Is she camped here?"

"No, never seen her before. Well, I'll have Jim stop down this afternoon." She got up from the table and returned everything to the tote.

"Oh, I didn't mean to impose..."

"No problem. Sunday afternoons are usually slow. Most of the people who are leaving today are already gone. And he *loves* to talk about it. See you later." Frannie almost expected to see puffs of smoke or streaks behind her as she left. Her constant energy made Frannie very tired.

So for the next hour she napped a lot and read a little. During one nap, she dreamt of a huge scary character

116

and managed to wake herself up only to be staring up at a giant with bushy hair and a beard, reminding her of Hagrid in the Harry Potter books.

CHAPTER ELEVEN

SUNDAY AFTERNOON

Frannie almost choked and tried to sit up too fast, resulting in a side spasm.

"Yes?" She didn't think she stammered too badly. At the same time her phone rang. The giant backed off and motioned for her to take it. She wasn't about to argue. She grabbed for the phone on the table, fumbling for the right button.

"Hello?" Her voice squeaked.

"Frannie? Are you okay? Where are you?" It was Larry.

"I'm right where you left me—in my chair." She couldn't take her eyes off the man in front of her. He wore baggy jeans and a flannel shirt that didn't quite meet at the bottom. His hair, beard and eyebrows would be overkill in Hollywood.

"You sound funny."

"I'm…fine. Where are you?" She tried to keep her voice even, but could hear it wasn't working.

"We're just loading the bikes to head back—should be there in half an hour or so. You're sure everything is okay?"

"Yes,...I have a visitor. See you soon." She hung up. "Have we met?"

"I'm Jim Larson, the owner."

Relief flooded through her. "Oh! Mary Louise's husband?"

He laughed, his whole body shaking, and she wondered why she had found him threatening. "We've only been married six months, and even though I've been the owner for years, I am now just 'Mary Louise's husband.' She said you had some questions about the old power plant."

"I do. Please sit down." She motioned at a lawn chair. "I've been fascinated by that place every time we come up here. Your wife said there's a tunnel, too?"

"You bet! A thousand feet long and all dug by candlelight."

"That's amazing. Is it still there?"

He nodded. "Now they only check it to monitor the bat population. They closed up the lower part of the entrance upriver when they shut down the power plant. When it was operating, the river was completely diverted through the plant. So in order for the river to return to its natural course, they had to prevent water from going down the tunnel."

She felt let down. "Oh."

"There's still some water that goes through it, but you can get into it from either end if you're determined enough."

"Oh," she said, seeing more possibilities again. "Mary Louise said there's stories about bootleggers using it at one time."

Jim leaned back in his chair and pulled a pipe out of his jeans' pocket and held it up. "Mind?"

She shook her head. Jim fiddled with the pipe for a few minutes, getting it lit and leaned back again.

"Oh, there's no doubt about that. When I was a kid, me and my buddies used to sneak down there. We found parts of wooden crates and even a bottle or two. I guess that's not absolute proof but it makes sense."

"So the tunnel goes west, then? From the plant?"

"Almost straight west. Runs right under the nature center."

"So where's the entrance?"

"Did you see the road to the bird watching station when you were at the center?" She nodded. "If you follow that down to the river, the entrance is right there. Used to be a dam there but it's been removed. Then the exit at the other end comes right into the power plant so the water could run the turbine. What are you planning, anyway?" He raised his eyebrows and puffed on his pipe.

She laughed. "Nothing, honest. When those women were killed yesterday, it happened just a few minutes before we got there. But we never met anyone when we were going down there. So how did the murderer get away?"

"Ahhh," said Jim. "But not many people know about the tunnel. I don't think there's been much interest in many years. Why do you think your murderer would know? You think it's someone from around here?"

"I have no idea. But I just can't figure any other way they could have gotten away. The tunnel might explain that." She looked over at the road as Larry's and Ben's trucks pulled in. Larry jumped out of his with a look of concern on his face, but relaxed into a grin when he saw Jim Larson.

"Jim!" He held out his hand. "Did you come to check on my invalid wife?"

"No, she just—"

"Mary Louise sent him down to entertain me with stories about the area around here," Frannie interrupted.

"You sounded funny on the phone," Larry said.

"I had just woke up when Jim stopped and then you called. I was pretty disoriented and I didn't know who Jim was."

"Well, I'd better get on with my chores." Jim winked at Frannie, emptied his pipe into the fire pit, and stuck it back in his pocket. "See you later."

As they watched him go, Frannie explained further to Larry. "I had never met him and when I woke up to see him standing over me, it scared me to death! You should have told me that Mary Louise's husband looks like Gentle Ben."

"I didn't realize that you'd never met. Even when we were up here before?"

Frannie shook her head. "Him I would remember. How was the ride?"

"Excellent," said Mickey. "We stopped for lunch at a little tavern in McCormick, but the best part was that it was all downhill. Literally. Lots of talk everywhere about the murders."

"So what did you do all day?" Jane Ann asked.

"Well, let's see. The sheriff was here, a TV reporter, the sheriff and deputies again to take the twins' trailer, then Mary Louise, then Jim." She ticked them all off on her fingers.

"A TV reporter?" Larry looked concerned again.

"Relax, dear—I told her I didn't know anything and then the deputies showed up to move the trailer so she and her sidekick had to get out of here."

"Anything new on the murder front?" Jane Ann said.

"Sorenson was mainly looking for info about last night. But she did say that the one twin—Virginia, we think—was hit on the side of the head and knocked into the machinery. The other, Valerie, was strangled."

"Really?" Donna plopped down in the chair beside her. "That's weird."

Frannie agreed.

"'We think?'" Larry repeated. "I thought you were staying out of this."

"I am. But you were there with me when Mary Sorenson first looked at the bodies and we talked about which twin was which."

"But why would a murderer hit one of them and strangle the other?" Donna said.

Larry started to say something but closed his mouth again.

122

"What?" Frannie asked.

"Nothing." He turned and went to put his bike behind the trailer.

Frannie's antenna went up. He knew something that he wasn't sharing. Just because he was an ex-cop, Sorenson probably told him something in confidence. Hmmm.

Donna and Jane Ann retired to their respective trailers for a rest. Larry returned and said he planned to watch golf.

"I thought we had a date," Frannie said.

"A date? Oh, the pie shop. Didn't you have any lunch?"

"I had a *lovely* lunch that Mary Louise brought me. We could go later, after golf."

"Okay, we can—," he stopped and looked at his watch. "No, let's go now."

Frannie's eyebrows went up at the change of heart, especially since golf was concerned. "You sure?"

"I'm sure. You deserve a reward for staying here all day."

"True." She grinned and levered herself out of her chair.

At the Pie Shoppe, Frannie chose lemon meringue while Larry ordered another piece of apple.

"You're in a rut," she told him.

"I know what I like."

They each got a cup of coffee as well and carried their purchases to a wooden booth. Being Sunday afternoon, the place was empty and the woman at the counter had the radio tuned to a country station while she cleaned up from the onslaught of weekend cyclists.

"So," Frannie said, savoring the creamy tang of the lemon, "what do you know that you aren't saying?"

He sipped his coffee and paused a minute. "That's why I thought we should get away for a bit. Sorenson told me last night that the little backpack she found by the door to that other room, you know? There was no ID, but there was a handgun in it."

Frannie sat up straight in surprise. "Larry, you old meddler, you!"

"I haven't changed my mind. I don't want you actively involved in this or any other investigation. But you seem to have an instinct for this and just wondered what your take is on it. Just don't mention it to anyone else for the time being."

She decided not to gloat over this small victory. She didn't want to be *actively* involved, but the puzzle of it intrigued her.

"Sorenson is sure the backpack belonged to one of the twins?"

"Fairly sure. The keys to their trailer were in it. She's checking to see if the gun is registered."

"So one of them came to the power plant with a gun — maybe carries it all the time, but maybe just expected to need it on this occasion. And yet didn't use it. She must not have felt threatened by whoever the murderer is."

"Apparently not."

"It appeared to me that Virginia, if she was the one hit on the head, died first, because of the way they were laying. What do you think?"

He nodded. "That's the way it looked."

"So maybe the gun belonged to her. If it belonged to Val, wouldn't she have tried to get it when her sister was attacked?"

"You would think so, but maybe she didn't have time or was too frightened to think about it. When you saw one of them leave that morning, did you see a backpack?"

"Definitely not. Just the camera bag."

"So we think one must have hiked and she had the backpack."

Frannie agreed. "Seems like it had to be that way. Whoever the gun is registered to must have been the one that hiked."

"Not necessarily. It could have been registered to one, but they both used it or at least knew about it."

She sighed. "You're right. Here's another weird thing. Yesterday when I walked to the restrooms in the afternoon, that guy Richard was sitting outside, so I stopped to give him my condolences. He claimed he hardly knew them; even acted like he barely remembered which one he met on the cruise. Yet, the night before, when he and Val were in a clinch on the road, he didn't seem to be having memory problems." She paused and grinned. "But, on the other hand, he also didn't seem to recognize me even though I was walking with Val before he called out to her."

"Really?" He contemplated that over a bite of pie. "Just because he had a fling that he doesn't want to admit to, doesn't make a motive for a double murder."

"I know. I can't figure that either. I'm more inclined to think the camera bag is the key. They said they took pictures of the old trailer and also at the nature center, but I can't imagine a motive there unless they have that crabby receptionist accepting a bribe or something."

He looked at her and smirked. "A bribe? For what?"

"Just thinking out of the box."

"Looks like a storm moving in," the counter woman called over her shoulder as she stood looking out one of the west windows. Frannie and Larry both looked over and realized it had certainly gotten darker.

He stacked his coffee cup on his plate. "You done?"

"Unless I lick my plate but I know that would be tacky."

"Mickey would do it."

They took their dishes to the bin, said goodbye to the counter woman, and headed back to the truck. Frannie managed to get in with a minimum of grunts and contortions. They were just crossing the bridge when a crash of thunder heralded a downpour.

Larry leaned forward slightly and peered through the thrashing wipers. "If this keeps up, it will put a damper, so to speak, on cooking supper." They had planned to grill barbecued chicken thighs.

"We could cook the chicken inside in the electric skillet."

"Could," he said. "Or we could just get wild and eat out."

"Mickey's probably already got a place spotted," she said.

"How are you feeling? You seem to be moving a little better."

"It *is* better. Kind of like a stitch in the side from running. Well, I think so. Been a long time since I ran anywhere."

"The junkyard at Bluffs last fall," he reminded her.

"Oh. Yeah."

When they pulled into their campsite, the fire circle was of course deserted and lights glowed in each of the campers. They sprinted for their own unit, or at least Larry did, Frannie following more slowly, holding an old brochure over her head. They had just gotten inside when Larry's phone rang. From the insults Larry flung at that innocent bit of technology, it was either a telemarketer or Mickey. Since the call ended with a discussion of a suppertime, it must be Mickey. Larry frequently carried on long conversations with telemarketers but almost never had supper with them.

He hung up. "That was Mickey."

"Uh-huh."

"He's proposing a road trip for supper." Mickey followed diner and restaurant shows on TV; his choices were usually spot-on.

"Something from one of his shows?"

127

"Not this time. He's suggesting Farrell's tavern where that floozie does her singing. Actually, he said Mary Louise says the food is excellent."

"Wow. That should be interesting. How soon?" Frannie said.

"About an hour and a half. The others are all on board."

"Great. Time for a little nap. I've had an exhausting day. It's been at least two hours since my last snooze." She kicked off her shoes and put them in the shoe cubby, grabbed a fleece throw, and headed to the bedroom.

"Well, those brain cells take energy, too, you know. I'll wake you about fifteen minutes before we go, okay?"

"Sure."

She slept for an hour and when she got up, found Larry comfortably snoozing the recliner, the golf tournament on TV struggling bravely on without him.

CHAPTER TWELVE
SUNDAY EVENING

With directions from Mary Louise, they found the tavern easily enough. It stood clustered with two other old wooden storefronts, the remnants of an abandoned town, optimistically located a century ago on an expected railroad route that never materialized. The inside featured worn wooden floors, mismatched chairs and Formica tables, an assortment of beer signs providing most of the dim lighting, and a dull roar of voices and laughter. They pushed a couple of tables together and perused the plastic menus propped between a pitted chrome napkin dispenser and a couple of disreputable looking salt and pepper shakers.

"Nice place," Larry said to Mickey with a smirk. "I forgot my tie."

"Food's supposed to be good," Mickey retorted.

Donna eyed a sticky spot on the table in front of her. "Anyone bring any wipes?"

Jane Ann laughed and Donna said, "I'm serious. Anybody have any?"

"I'm sure the waitress will wipe the tables off for us," Nancy said in a low voice.

"Well, I'm not eating off it this way," Donna said. She leaned back in her chair, crossed her arms, and looked around for said waitress.

With none in sight, Rob went to the bar and returned with a wet rag. He wiped both tables, and draping the rag over his arm, said to his wife, "Would madame care for an aperitif before ordering?"

Donna was not amused. All she said was, "I hope the kitchen is cleaner than the rest of the place."

"Oh, they don't have a kitchen," Mickey said. "They cook it all in back by the outhouse."

"Out—? Mickey, you're just putting me on," Donna loosened up a little and even gave a forced smile.

"Mickey?" Ben said. "Never."

The menu consisted entirely of baskets. Shrimp baskets, chicken baskets, hamburger baskets, tenderloin baskets. Also offered were baskets of appetizers: deep-fried mushrooms, cauliflower, cheese, pickles, zucchini, and jalapeños. By the time they had all made their choices, a gaunt and grizzled waitress appeared at the table, older than any of them by at least a decade. Her weathered face, framed in frizzy grey hair, evidenced many years of smiles and sadness.

"Getcha?" she said.

They gave their orders while she glanced between them and other patrons. She wrote nothing down, just nodding from time to time. As she hurried away, Ben said, "No way we're all going to get what we ordered."

"I don't know." Nancy watched the woman push through a swinging door in the back. "She looks pretty seasoned."

"Salty, you mean?" Mickey commented.

While Larry and Rob got pitchers of beer and soda and a tray of mugs and glasses, Frannie scrutinized the tavern. Most of the patrons appeared to be locals who knew each other well. In the front far corner, she noticed familiar faces. "I think that's the guys from the old trailer by the campground," she whispered to Jane Ann. At a round table in the shadows, backs to the wall, were the older scruffy guy and the skinhead. "According to Mary Louise, Mel something and his son, Dale."

"Probably here to see Ms. Rump," Jane Ann said. While they were waiting for their food, the skinhead got up and slouched past them to the restroom. His jeans looked well past their laundry date and the tight black t-shirt sported symbols and a logo unfamiliar to Frannie— she assumed some heavy metal group. His arms bore several complex tattoos and he looked straight ahead as he passed.

The food arrived, baskets and baskets of it. The 'baskets' of course were plastic ones, in primary colors, but, contrary to their expectations, every order was correct. Frannie, not a great fan of fried food, was delighted that her shrimp was not over-breaded or over-fried. It really was good.

They were just finishing when another familiar figure walked by their tables.

"Hey! Y'all did come out to hear me! Bless you. Ah'm jes tickled pink." Frannie groaned inwardly in embarrassment for the woman. She looked up first into the structured chest, on up to the top of an even more structured hairdo.

"Well, we heard the food was good here, too, so it's a double bonus, sort of."

"Sure is. Welcome! Hope y'all enjoy the show." Jonie squinted her eyes and lifted one shoulder in what she thought of as a coquettish gesture. As she sashayed through the room blessing this customer and being tickled pink by that one, Frannie said in a whisper only loud enough for her group to hear, "Country singers don't really look like that any more, do they?"

Rob shook his head. "Maybe that's why she is still waiting for a call."

But later, they decided that it wasn't only her style of dress that kept her in Minnesota. Her voice wasn't bad, but by the time she added her cheesy accent and her impression of several country stars, the quality of her voice was lost. The group stayed through the first set and decided to leave during Jonie's break. The rain had let up and they were all eager to get back and relax in more comfortable chairs around a fire.

The men slipped a few bills into the tip jar on the bar, and they were almost out the door when a loud crash to the right distracted them.

It was the skinhead kid, confronting a large red-headed young man.

"Shut yer mouth!" screamed the skinhead in a high-pitched voice, leaning across an overturned chair.

The bartender, a wizened guy who appeared to be in his seventies and could have been a brother to the waitress, hurried over to break it up.

He started to say, "Hey, Dale, cool it..." Dale swung around, fists up, to take on this new opposition, but lowered his fists a bit when he saw the bartender. His face was still twisted with anger at whatever the redhead had said, but he wasn't about to hit an old man.

Mel Dubrak reached the confrontation by then and put his hand on his son's shoulder. Dale shook it off.

"Leave me alone, old man! You're just like the rest of 'em." He twisted away and stormed out the door.

As the bartender headed back to his station, Frannie said, "What was that about?"

The bartender looked at the closing door, wiping his hands on the towel he carried. "Oh, young Dubrak thinks he's some kind of revolutionary. Sees conspiracy everywhere and some folks like to say things to stir him up." He shrugged. "Just local entertainment."

Frannie's group continued out the door. Dale Dubrak had his hand on the door handle of the old gray pickup when Mel opened the bar door and yelled, "You ain't takin' that truck. Find your own way back." He closed the door without waiting to see if his son obeyed him.

Dale glared at the closed door and started to trudge down the gravel road. Frannie was struggling to follow Nancy into the crew seat of the Terells' pickup when Ben called out to the young man's retreating back.

"If you're going back to the campground, we can give you a ride."

Dale walked a few more steps and slowly turned around, eyes narrowed.

"You'd have to ride in the back," Ben continued as Dale shuffled back toward them. The young man shrugged, but Frannie said, "That isn't necessary, Ben. I can slide over. Nancy only takes up as much space as half a person anyway."

Ben looked in the open window at her. "Are you sure? You don't need to be jostled around."

"I'm fine," she fudged a little on the truth. She *was* looking forward to her recliner, but for a few miles she could survive.

Larry held the passenger door open so Dale could climb in the back. He hugged the door, keeping a space between him and Frannie. "Thanks," he mumbled.

Once in, Ben pulled the pickup out to follow Rob and Donna's truck. Frannie turned to their rider and said, "I'm Frannie Shoemaker. Do you live with your dad?"

He looked at her, surprised apparently that anyone would want to speak to him, and said, "Just for a while."

"What do you do?"

"Excuse me?"

"I mean, are you working, or going to school, or what?"

He looked out the window. "I'm training."

"Oh," she said brightly. "For the military or a marathon or something?"

He looked at her again with hooded eyes, said, "Something like that," gave a half smile and turned back to the window.

Since there was nothing to see in the dark countryside, Frannie took the hint and remained silent the rest of the short trip. When they reached the campground, Dale leaped out of the truck at the first opportunity, looked directly at Ben and thanked him, ignoring the others. He took off in an easy lope cutting through the campground toward the old trailer at the end.

"What an odd duck," Nancy said, watching him go.

"He wasn't very forthcoming about what he is training for," Frannie said.

"Probably just an excuse for doing nothing," Ben said. "He doesn't give me the impression that he's very ambitious."

Mickey and Larry were busy building a fire and, of course, arguing about it, while Rob and Jane Ann got out lawn chairs. Once seated, Frannie told them all what she had learned from Jim about the tunnel.

"So it's still accessible?" Rob asked.

"That's what he said. He said you can see the entrance from the bird watching area at the nature center. I'd like to see that. We didn't get to see much of the center on Saturday."

Larry looked at her with narrowed eyes, but Rob jumped in. "I'd like to try one of the high ropes courses. Maybe we should go back there in the morning. And we never did get to do any of the trails."

Jane Ann studied a brochure that she had picked up on their visit to the center. "This map shows a 'Night Sensory Course' out behind the Visitor's Center. I wonder what that is?"

Mickey started to open his mouth, but she gave him a look and said, "Don't even say it."

"Afterwards, we could go have lunch at that wooden diner in Burdensville," Donna said.

"And maybe shop a little?" Rob grinned at his wife.

"Maybe. Just a little," Donna answered.

"We should've stopped at the pie shop on our way home and gotten some pie for dessert," Ben said.

"Oh!" Donna jumped up, knocking over her chair. "I have fresh strawberries and we picked up ice cream yesterday in Burdensville. I almost forgot!"

After a little round of applause, Rob and Donna headed across the road to their camper. The golf cart puttered up as they reached the road, driven by Jim this time with Mary Louise and the cat riding shotgun. Donna invited them for ice cream and they eagerly accepted.

While they waited, Frannie and Larry filled the owners in on the events of the evening at Farrell's.

Mary Louise shook her head in disgust. "That Dale! Sometimes I wonder if he didn't join some cult or something. He did quit drinking and that's a blessing, but he's always spouting stuff about imperialists and the downtrodden. He spends a lot of time on the high ropes course over at the nature center and at the shooting range."

"He said he's 'training,' but wouldn't say what for," Frannie said. "Just gave a funny little smile, like it's a secret or something."

Mary Louise shrugged. "I'm not sure I even want to know."

Rob and Donna arrived back with bowls of ice cream and strawberries. As usual, the group was easily distracted by food. While she ate, Frannie thought about Dale Dubrak and why he might be so secretive. But when she finished she said to Mary Louise, "I didn't notice when we drove in. Is Richard still here?"

"Yup, 'sposed to be here all week. Jim says he comes every year to bike the trail. Great dessert, by the way. Haven't had many fresh strawberries yet this season. How are you feeling?"

"Better. Hurts if I turn too quickly, or we hit a bump in the truck, and I feel pretty winded a lot of the time, but a lot better than yesterday at this time."

"Great!"

They quizzed Jim about the tunnel and its history, especially during the prohibition years. Finally Rob collected the bowls and spoons, the Larsons putted away in the golf cart, and the rest began dispersing to their campers. Mickey and Larry launched into a discussion of the baseball season.

Once inside, Frannie opened her laptop, which she kept charging on the dinette table. She did a search for 'Ellis-Reynolds Chicago.' She found several references to Richard and the securities firm he worked for. She typed in a search on the firm and found recent articles about an investigation but no names were mentioned in those. Another search on just Reynolds and Chicago yielded some historical information, mostly about prohibition. A man named Herbert Reynolds had been actively involved in bootlegging operations. Now, that was an interesting coincidence.

She closed out of that and checked the weather for the next day as Larry came in with Cuba.

"What's it look like?" he said, looking over her shoulder at the radar map.

"Good," she said, closing the laptop. "No rain for tomorrow." She eased herself out of the bench seat.

"Excellent. I'm turning in."

"Me too," she said. And they did.

CHAPTER THIRTEEN
MONDAY MORNING

Monday morning was crisp, clear, and on the cool side. As they entered the grounds of the nature center, Larry, in the lead, turned down a road marked with a sign that read "Bird Watching Area." The narrow track followed the slope down toward the river and ended in a small parking lot. A railing divided the parking lot from a heavily wooded eight or ten-foot drop down to the river. The trees and shrubs had been cleared in an area about twenty feet wide to provide a view of the river.

To the side of the lot was a three-sided wooden structure, open to the lot with a long bench and a high rectangular opening away from the lot that looked out onto the bluff. They walked over and discovered laminated posters on the walls identifying the birds native to the area. Outside the opening, various types of bird feeders were hung in the trees and were being frequented by a greater variety of birds than Frannie had ever seen out in the open in one place.

They observed in awe, poking each other and naming varieties that they recognized in hushed tones.

"Didn't anyone bring binoculars?" Ben asked.

"Oh! I did!" Frannie pulled a small pair out of her backpack and handed them to Ben.

He scanned a group of pines down the slope a little ways. "I thought so. There's a cedar waxwing in those evergreens. We don't see those often." He handed the glasses back to Frannie and pointed in the general direction. She aimed the binoculars and, after some adjustment and moving slowly up and down and back and forth, saw the yellow-bellied bird in the branches of an old twisted juniper, nibbling what appeared to be raisins and berries from a flat wooden platform.

"Isn't he beautiful?" she breathed.

"I wanna see!" Sometimes Donna sounded like a five-year-old. Frannie looked a little longer and as she panned away from the bird, caught sight of an opening in the side of the bluff near the water.

"Wait a minute," she said, moving the glasses out of Donna's reach and losing the view of the opening. When she focused in on it again, she said. "I think maybe that's the upstream entrance to the tunnel. Jim Larson said you could see it from here."

Larry said, "Show me." Frannie handed him the glasses, ignoring Donna's almost pathetic face. She gave Larry directions to find what she had seen.

"I think you're right. Looks like it would be pretty hard to get down there from here." He passed the glasses to Donna, who then grudgingly handed them to the others after a couple of minutes. Frannie thought about what Larry said and then returned to the open view in the parking lot. She stood looking down at the river until Larry joined her.

"Now what, Sherlock?"

"When we were on that memorable float the other day, the last time we stopped I think was right down there on that point."

"Yeah?"

"Remember when I was waiting, I said I saw Richard and his girlfriend or whatever and they kept disappearing? I think they had gotten out right below here."

"I still don't get it."

"I wonder if they were going into the tunnel."

"Why would they?"

"Last night I did a search on his name. There was a Reynolds in Chicago connected to the prohibition era and bootlegging. Maybe it was a relative and Richard had heard stories growing up."

He shook his head. "But the DNR is in there regularly, and if there was anything left from those days in there, they would have found it long ago. Besides, Richard has been here many times. He probably just found the tunnel exploring."

"Could be."

The rest of the group had joined them and decided to continue on to the Visitor's Center. They boarded the vehicles again and headed back up the narrow road, hoping they wouldn't meet anyone.

At the Center, Frannie was relieved to see that a young blonde woman was behind the reception desk rather than the formidable Deborah McCabe.

"Hi!" she said, smiling brightly. Her name tag read 'Sara Hermanson.' "Can I help you?" Yes, a definite change in the atmosphere.

"We're interested in all of your programs here," Mickey said. "Like what is the 'Night Sensory Course?'"

"Oh," Sara laughed. "Everyone wonders about that. There is a length of rope and it might run along a tree, across a log on the ground, around a stump, and like that, y'know? People pair off and one person is blindfolded." She mimed putting a blindfold on and then grasping an imaginary rope. "The blindfolded person hangs onto the rope and tries to figure out where they are and what they are touching as they go along. Their partner follows along to make sure they don't get hurt. It's really cool. People learn to listen and use their other senses besides their eyes." She took a breath. "If you would like to try it, we are having an open house tonight to get more people familiar with what we offer here."

Mickey said. "That sounds great. What time?"

"It starts at 7:00. It won't be dark enough for the night course until about 8:30 but you can check out the other challenges until then."

"So we know about the high ropes courses. What else do you have?" Rob said.

"All kinds of stuff. There's an obstacle course, a zip line, a rock climbing wall, and you can try archery if you want. Here's a flyer that lists everything and also has a small map." She passed out one apiece from a large stack.

Director Lindorf heard them and came out of his office. "Glad to see you back again. I hope this visit ends better than the last one. How are you all?"

"We're fine," Larry said. "Well, most of us. Frannie took a fall canoeing the other day and is pretty sore."

"Oh, my," he said, looking at her with sympathy. "That's not what we want, is it?"

Frannie shook her head, feeling like she was his niece or granddaughter and a delinquent one, at that. Larry went on, "We're thinking of coming back tonight for your open house."

Lindorf clapped his hands. "Great! You need to try the zip line." He looked at Frannie again. "Well, maybe not you, Mrs. Shoemaker."

Surprised that he remembered her name, Frannie shook her head again. "I wouldn't anyway. I'm afraid of heights."

"No loss, then," he smiled. "I must run. Another meeting, I'm afraid." He nodded, and headed down a hallway to the back of the building.

The group went back outside to decide how much looking around they wanted to do before lunch. Rob wanted to hike down to a restored Indian encampment and pointed out the route on the map. Frannie looked over toward the edge of the woods and spotted two people leaning toward each other in heated discussion. One was Deborah McCabe and the other was Dale Dubrak.

"Hmmm," she mumbled to Nancy. "That's an interesting pair."

"It hardly looks like they're friends," Nancy said.

"No…, but I get the impression that they know each other pretty well. He's not just taking a reprimand from her."

McCabe noticed them looking and straightened up into her officious posture. She then appeared to be giving him directions and he glanced over at Frannie's group too and then took off down the trail. McCabe strode back toward the Visitor's Center.

"Strange bedfellows," said Nancy.

Frannie gave her a sideways look. "Surely not."

"I just mean like the old saying 'Politics makes strange bedfellows.'"

"Neither one of them strike me as being very political," Frannie said.

"Mary Louise did say Dale is always 'spouting off about imperialists' and we've never actually had a conversation with Miss Congeniality."

"Girls! Get with the program," Mickey interrupted. "We're going to try the trail to the Indian encampment."

"Okay," said Frannie. "I need to get my sunglasses and water bottle from the truck first."

After dropping off excess baggage and picking up hiking supplies at the vehicles, they started down a trail that sloped gently and was wide and well-maintained. Their pace was slow and easy, in deference to Frannie's injury and Mickey's tendency to get easily winded.

At the bottom of a ravine, they crossed a quaint wooden bridge and followed the trail, gradually rising between a bluff on one side and small stream on the other. Tall, skinny birches reached up for the sun and resilient wildflowers and ferns clung to the side of the bluff. She was reminded of a hike along a stream at Bat Cave State Park that ended with finding a body in a cave. She shivered.

"You okay, Frannie?" came Jane Ann's voice behind her.

Frannie gave a wry little laugh. "This path reminds me of the one in Bat Cave Park when we found Maeve Schlumm."

"You've already found two bodies this weekend—I think that's your quota. We shouldn't run into any more."

"Let's hope so."

The trail had climbed about twenty feet above the stream and the last ten feet or so were steeper, leading to a clearing at the top of the bluff. Three small bark lodges were arranged around a fire ring. Frannie was excited by the sight. During her years of teaching social studies, she had spent considerable time every year covering the various Native American cultures. How great it would have been to bring kids to a place like this.

They wandered around the site, examining the heavy iron pot over the fire and hides drying on a rack. Frannie lifted the flap on one of the lodges to peer inside, gasped, and lurched back.

Nancy said, "What is it?"

"Someone's in there...laying down..."

Larry bent over and pulled the flap back, stared a minute, and straightened up.

She waited, holding her breath.

"It's okay. She's not real. It's a manikin of an Indian woman."

"Oh!" She sat down on a stump. "Oh! We just talked about finding a body at Bat Cave and I thought...," She gave them all a sheepish grin and pushed her hair behind her ears, taking as deep a breath as she could manage.

Donna, who just had a look for herself, said, "Why would they have a manikin sleeping? I mean, those things aren't cheap. You'd think they'd have her doing something, like cooking."

"You can ask Deborah when we get back," Nancy said with a smirk.

"Right. I'm sure she'd be helpful."

Mickey looked at his watch. "Getting close to lunch time. Better head back."

"We don't have to worry about missing meals with Mickey around," Rob said.

"Hey, that's my line," Larry protested.

They took the path back single file, Larry helping Frannie down the steeper part. At the parking lot, several paused for swigs of water and Ben sat down on a bench to retie his shoe. Sara, the young woman who had been at the reception desk came out of the Visitor's Center swinging a purse and jingling her car keys.

"Hi!" she called out. "Did you hike one of the trails?"

"We did," Nancy said. "We went to see the Indian encampment. It's very nice but we were wondering why they would put a manikin lying down in one of the lodges."

Sara laughed, a merry tinkling sound. "She doesn't stand up very well. So when we have tours or open houses like tonight, we'll prop her up by the hides when we explain brain tanning. Otherwise they put her in a lodge so she doesn't get knocked over."

Frannie nodded but Donna said, "Brain tanning?"

"They used brain matter to soften the hides," Frannie said. "Animal brains," she added seeing the look on Donna's face.

"I will never wear another pair of moccasins," Donna said.

"Are you done for the day? Or just on lunch break?" Ben asked Sara.

"I'll be back to help tonight. I work Monday mornings so Deborah can have some time off. Run errands, that sort of thing."

"We saw her before we started the hike," Frannie said. "She appeared to be arguing with that young Dale Dubrak."

"Arguing?" Sara looked puzzled. "She's kind of taken Dale under her wing, supervises him on the obstacle course and that sort of thing."

"He said last night that he's training, but wouldn't say for what," Frannie pushed, ignoring Larry's signals that they were ready to leave.

Sara shrugged. "I think Dale's just a big talker. Doesn't seem to want to work. Well, I have to pick up my little boy from the sitter. Have a good day!" She waved and slid into the driver's seat of an old compact Honda.

"Frannie..." Larry said, a warning tone in his voice. "Meddle, meddle, meddle."

"I'm just curious," she answered as they walked to the truck.

"Right."

The wooden diner sat on its wheels in a pocket park space between two old brick buildings on the main street of Burdensville. It sported a cream and forest green paint job with dark red accents. Larry was the first up the steps and pulled open an old-fashioned screen door. He turned back to the group. "Standing room only."

"There's picnic tables out behind," Jane Ann pointed out. "We could get carry-out."

He nodded. "I'll get some menus." There were just a few customers at the picnic tables, so they settled around an open one. Donna brushed crumbs off while the rest examined the outside of the unique little restaurant. Larry returned with a handful of menus on newsprint with an old railroad timetable printed on the front.

"Lots of interesting-looking sandwiches, and it says all the bread is homemade," Nancy said. They made their decisions, Frannie settling on a chicken salad sandwich with apples, walnuts, and cranberries and a raspberry iced tea. The men went back in to place the orders, so

Frannie got up to walk around. She didn't want to sit on the bench any longer than necessary.

Old bricks surfaced the courtyard with planting areas left open. A couple of medium-sized maples shaded the area and interesting combinations of grasses, crotons, red salvia, and lime green sweet potato vine filled the planters. She noticed an attractive dark-haired woman waiting alone at a small round table and nodded to her as she passed.

"Say!" the woman said. "Weren't you on the float trip the other day?" Frannie looked at her more closely. It was the woman who had been with Richard.

"Yes, I was. I think you were with Richard?"

"Sure thing. He always wants to camp but I'm not much for roughing it so I stay at a nearby B & B."

"You've been here before, then?"

"Every year for the last four or five years. Like I said, I don't do the biking, hiking, and camping thing, but I did agree to the canoe float. It was okay but I was sure glad to get back to my shower. My name's Claire, by the way."

Frannie introduced herself and pointed out her group.

"This is such a cute town. Great shops, even a couple of upscale ones." Claire was probably also amazed that there was even electricity out here in the sticks. "Here comes my lunch! Nice to meet you."

Frannie looked up to see Richard weaving through the tables with a tray. She said goodbye to Claire and, as she walked back to her group, noticed Richard watching her. No wonder. Four or five years he's been coming here with Claire? Apparently Claire went her own way enough of the time that he thought he could pull off a rendezvous or two with Valerie. Scumbag, she thought again.

She didn't believe for a minute his protestations about not knowing Val. If it had only been Val's brief confidential revelation, she would be more skeptical, but she had witnessed Richard with Val. He was a liar. But would that have been enough motive for murder? Even if it was, why kill both twins? To make sure he got the right one?

"Earth to Frannie," Jane Ann said.

"Sorry, just thinking," she said as she sat back down.

"That's never good. Have you got those murders solved?"

"Not even close."

The men returned with trays laden with brown paper wrapped sandwiches and paper boxes full of sweet potato fries.

"By the time we're done, the crowd should be cleared out. You girls need to check out the inside of that place — completely restored," Rob said.

"And they have strawberry-rhubarb pie," Larry added.

"Who were you talking to, Frannie?" Donna mumbled around a mouth full of tenderloin.

"The woman who was canoeing with Richard the other day."

150

Jane Ann looked over her shoulder at the pair who were deep in conversation across the courtyard. "I didn't recognize her."

"I didn't either at first," Frannie said. "She asked me if I was on the float trip. Her name is Claire. Seems she and Richard have been coming here for *several* years."

Jane Ann raised her eyebrows. "Really." It wasn't a question. "So maybe Val misinterpreted his intentions?"

"His intentions, I think, were to lead her along as long as he could. So in that sense, yes, she was misinterpreting. I wonder now if he didn't decide it was more expedient to get rid of her. Especially with Claire here at the same time."

"You think *Richard* is the murderer?" Nancy said.

Larry put his sandwich down and took a drink of his tea. "Don't spread that around. If you're wrong, you could be in for a lawsuit, and if you're right, you'll put yourself at risk again," he admonished Frannie quietly.

"I know." She rolled up her sandwich paper and started on her fries. "These are fantastic. Great sandwich too. Good suggestion, Donna."

Donna smiled smugly. "You guys don't listen to me often enough."

When they finished, they dumped their trash in a nearby barrel and trooped inside. The crowd had cleared out so they could admire the yellow-brown car siding on the walls, green and white checked tile floors, and Forties-era lunch counter and stools. Several got pieces of pie in carry-out containers for "later" and exited the diner.

Frannie caught her foot on the wooden steps and nearly somersaulted to another disaster, but a firm hand caught her arm. She looked up to thank her rescuer into the face of Richard. "Watch it," he said.

Chapter Fourteen
Monday Afternoon

Frannie was so startled, she couldn't think to respond until Richard had disappeared into the diner. Larry took her hand down the rest of the steps.

"What did he say to you?"

"To watch it."

"Watch your step, you mean?"

"I don't know. I suppose, but he almost sounded menacing."

"Could be your imagination since you've decided he's a murderer."

"I haven't decided anything. I just have a lot of questions about him." They had reached the trucks and he helped her in. Donna and Rob climbed in the back.

"We still have ice cream if you want some with your pie when we get back to the campground," Donna said.

"Sounds good," Frannie said. "And then I think I'm ready for a nap."

She slept a solid two hours and, when she woke, felt even groggier than before. She stretched and headed outside. Maybe a little exercise would be just the ticket.

Jane Ann sat at the picnic table, making a beaded bracelet.

"Where's everyone else?" Frannie said.

"Larry and Mickey went fishing. Rob wanted to try the ropes course; Donna said she'd go along if they could go back to Burdensville after so she could shop some more." Jane Ann actually snickered. "Poor Rob. I think Ben and Nancy went for a hike."

"I need some exercise," Frannie said. "I feel like a slug. Want to go for a little bike ride just around the campground?"

"Sure. Just let me put this away. The raccoons around here are so well fed, they'll be taking up hobbies next and I don't want them finishing this bracelet. In case you haven't noticed, raccoons don't have much taste."

Frannie laughed. "I'll leave a note for Larry."

Jane Ann came back out of their camper, pulling her blond hair back with a red scrunchie. Frannie stuck a bottle of water in the holder on her bike and they set off.

"Which way?" Jane Ann said when they got to the main road through the campground.

"Let's go ride through the loop where the seasonal campers are."

"Good idea."

They rode up toward the shower house and office and then turned off on a side road. There were a few more temporary campsites in this area, including Richard's. Another loop took them into the seasonal area. Tall pines and native shrubs separated many of the sites. Renters took more time to give a look of permanence to their sites, with flowers, lawn furniture, and ornaments. Many of the units belonged to people from Rochester or the Twin Cities, who came on weekends just as they would to a lake cabin.

Being a weekday, the loop was quiet. Frannie stopped when they got to the log cabin trailer. "Hold on a minute," she called to Jane Ann's back. Jane Ann turned in the road and peddled back. They leaned on their bikes and looked at the unusual unit. The owners had skirted the bottom with panels of lattice work to camouflage the wheels and water and sewer hookups. It looked quite permanent.

"Quite a camper, isn't it?" called a voice from the next unit. They both jumped.

A short woman with silver cropped hair worked cleaning and straightening a low deck made of interlocking wooden tiles. She had just leaned a broom against a lawn chair and was trying to move a large grill.

"It sure is," Jane Ann said. "Do you need some help?"

"I would love it!" the woman said. "One of the wheels broke and we haven't gotten it replaced."

Frannie and Jane Ann parked their bikes and walked over to the site. Jane Ann helped move the grill to the other edge of the deck.

The woman wiped her forehead with the back of her hand. "Thank you so much. Can I offer you a glass of tea?"

Jane Ann looked at Frannie. They both nodded. "Sounds good," Frannie said, "but we don't want to interrupt your work."

"I'm ready for a break," she said. "I'm Barb, by the way. Have a chair and I'll get it."

She soon returned with a tray of three tall glasses.

Frannie grinned after taking a drink. "We were ready for a break, too. We rode all the way from the other end of the campground."

Barb looked at her, puzzled a minute, and then chuckled. "Absolutely, that *is* strenuous. But I can't talk—I hardly get any regular exercise at all," she said. "I've been working all day to get this place ready for the summer. My family will be coming later this week for a visit. Amazing what accumulates over the winter."

Frannie and Jane Ann asked her about seasonal stays and then the talk returned to the log cabin trailer.

"Mary Louise said the people who own it, the Sturms, are supposed to be gone on an extended trip to Europe, but I'm sure I saw Mrs. Sturm leave last evening. I don't know her very well—we're not often here at the same time—but she had on this great batik shirt that I've seen her wear before," Barb said.

"Have you been inside?" Frannie asked.

"Just once. It's really cute."

They visited a while longer and then Jane Ann stood. "Thanks for the tea. We'll let you get back to your work."

"Thank *you* for the help. Just set your glasses on the tray, and stop back any time. I'm here by myself all week and it gets pretty lonely."

They agreed and mounted their bikes, waving as they pulled away. They continued around the loop, stopping to observe some fishermen on the river bank, and returned to their campsite.

"That was just what I needed," Frannie said. "I slept too long and was really stiff. I think I'm even ready to help with supper. What are we having?"

"Boy, you have been out of it! Donna rambled on this morning for ten minutes about the 'amazing' barbecued chicken she and Rob are doing for us tonight. Mickey and I are fixing some sautéed veggies and salad; Nancy has potato salad. We're covered so you're out of luck."

Frannie grinned. "I'm getting pretty good at tuning Donna out. But I didn't hear you mention dessert. What's with that?"

Jane Ann pulled her lawn chair into the shade and shrugged. "Sounded like we had plenty of food."

"Nonsense, when did that ever stop us? I'll do a peach cobbler. I've got whole frozen peaches in the freezer from last year."

"Welll…if you go to all the effort, I guess I won't pass it up."

"I'll just get them out to thaw."

She returned outside just in time to hear Mary Louise yoohooing. She chugged up in her golf cart almost right up to their chairs.

"Saw you go by on your bikes earlier." She looked at Frannie. "You feeling well enough to do that?"

"Mary Louise, between my husband, you, and Nurse Jane Fuzzy Wuzzy here, I don't stand a chance of overexerting. We just rode around the campground, down around the seasonal sites."

Mary Louise looked perplexed. "Nurse who?"

Jane Ann jumped in. "Frannie likes to throw in literary allusions whenever she can. Nurse Jane Fuzzy Wuzzy was a character in the Uncle Wiggly children's books popular in the *olden* days when we were growing up."

"Oh, I remember — the Uncle Wiggly game! Is that the same?"

"Yup, it was based on the books."

"Anyway," Frannie said, "I just love that log cabin trailer down there."

Mary Louise nodded, her red curls bouncing. "Sturms. They've been here several years, I guess. But they're gone to Europe right now."

Frannie shook her head. "The neighbor — Barb? — said she saw Mrs. Sturm last night."

Mary Louise looked stunned. "That can't be. They always check in when they come in and she told me they wouldn't be back until the middle of June."

"Barb seemed sure it was her because of the shirt she was wearing."

"I need to check this out. Want to go for a ride?"

Jane Ann and Frannie looked at each other and said, "Sure" in unison. Frannie climbed in the passenger seat while Jane Ann got in the back. Mary Louise took off with a lurch, Frannie let out an involuntary "Oof!", Mary Louise said, "Oh, sorry!" and slowed down.

Several jolts and jostles later they arrived at Barb's trailer. She was still sweeping and tidying her deck.

Mary Louise hopped out as soon as the cart rolled to a stop. Even though Frannie was much smaller than the campground owner, she realized as she gingerly swiveled out of the seat and clambered to her feet that she felt like she was twice Mary Louise's size and twice her own age — not easy.

"Hey, Barb!" Mary Louise boomed. Barb straightened and turned, breaking into a smile.

"I was just complaining to these two nice ladies that it was pretty lonely here by myself," she said coming forward to greet Mary Louise.

"Well, these two nice ladies were just telling me that you saw Georgia Sturm last night?"

"Yeah, I'm sure I did. It was close to dark, but, as I said to them," Barb dipped her head toward Frannie and Jane Ann, "she had on that really neat batik shirt — all blues and greens — that she wore a lot last summer."

Mary Louise tilted her head. "I remember that shirt. Have you seen lights on there at night?"

Barb thought a minute, looking at the trailer next door as if the answer could be seen there.

"I don't think so, but the trees sort of block it. Why? Is something wrong?"

"Sturms told me that they would be gone until the middle of June. What kind of car did she leave in?"

"She didn't. She walked down that way and I never saw her again. But I went in soon after that." Barb pointed at the east end of the campground.

"That's odd. Thanks. I think I'll check it out." She led the way around the end of the log cabin trailer and stepped on to a little porch on the side. She examined the door latch and then knocked on it. No response. She peered in through a very narrow space between a curtain and the door.

"Oh. My. God."

"What is it?" Frannie stood at the bottom of the steps with Jane Ann. Mary Louise hurried back down the steps as they parted to let her through.

"What?" Jane Ann insisted. "What did you see?"

"I think this is that meth source the cops have been looking for. Barb!" she called as they headed for the cart. "Why don't you come with us?"

"Where?"

"I'll explain on the way. Is anyone else in this area, do you know?"

Barb shook her head. "I haven't seen anyone." She and Jane Ann sat backwards in the cargo area, Frannie climbed in front, and Mary Louise started the cart and took off like a rocket. Frannie held her breath and clung to the side, trying to raise herself off the seat each time they neared a pothole to minimize the bumps.

On the way back to the office, Mary Louise yelled over her shoulder about what she had seen in the log cabin trailer.

"I think that's a meth lab in there!"

Barb said, "You mean the Sturms are making drugs?"

Mary Louise shook her head. "Not at all. I think someone's squatting in there. No one's been around the seasonal area much this spring. It would be easy to do."

Realization dawned on Barb. "And even wearing their *clothes*?"

"Why not?" Mary Louise gave a wry smile as she brought the cart to a halt by the office and pulled out her cell. "It's a cool shirt."

Frannie was puzzled. "Why didn't you just call from there?"

"Too dangerous. I wanted to get you all away from that place."

As realization of what Mary Louise said dawned on Barb, she turned pale. "Gosh, I've been right next door for two days."

After Mary Louise finished her call, Jane Ann and Frannie decided to walk back to their campsite. The only message they had left for the others said they were on a bike ride, and since their bikes were at the campsite, that communication could cause some question. Barb would wait with Mary Louise for the authorities.

By the time they reached their site, they could hear sirens approaching on the highway. Larry looked toward the highway and then at them.

"Now what did you two do?"

Jane Ann held up her hands. "Not us, sir. We have been little angels."

Larry raised his eyebrows and said, "Right." So Frannie filled him in on events at the log cabin trailer.

Frannie saw Larry's jaw drop for the first time in forty years. "I could have sworn it was that old trailer." He then attempted to save face, defending his earlier conclusions. "Of course, there could be one there too."

Frannie shrugged and smiled. "Possible. But can you imagine having someone living in *our* trailer—*wearing* our clothes? Ewww—as Sabet would say."

"Probably happens more than we know."

"How do they get in?"

"Like anywhere else. Pick a lock."

Jane Ann became serious. "Now what, Larry? Will they just stake out that place and see who comes back?"

"I don't think so. It's too dangerous to leave a lab in place with those other campers and more people coming in by the weekend."

The others had returned as well and story was repeated and the turn of events discussed ad nauseam since no one knew what was happening. After concluding that they knew nothing and therefore couldn't solve anything, they decided to fix supper.

They were almost finished eating when Mary Louise and Jim showed up in the golf cart. Both came over to the table.

Mary Louise shook her head. "Man! Not what I expected to do today!"

Jim took an offered chair and a beer. "Makes you wonder what else has gone on over there that we don't know about. I've heard of these squatting incidents but always scoffed—like, 'there'd be some signs, right? Somebody's not paying attention!' But we live here year 'round, and check that area all the time. Never saw a thing."

"Did they walk in? Surely they weren't there all the time?" Frannie asked.

"Cops found signs of a lot of traffic past the east end of the campground. There's a little parking lot near the bridge where a lot of people park when they're fishing. This outfit must have parked there and walked in. The cops don't think they were there all of the time but no one knows for sure."

"So, now what?" Ben said. "Have they removed all the apparatus?"

"Yup," Mary Louise said, "Boxed everything up and carted it out. They'll try and get fingerprints off it in the lab, I guess. Tomorrow a special crew will come in and clean it good. I had to try and contact the Sturms about what happened. It's late over there so I sent a text for them to call me. *That* won't be a fun conversation!" She tried to deny her words with laughter.

"I don't envy you," Nancy said.

"So, what's next on your agenda? Do I have more excitement to look forward to tonight?" Mary Louise said.

"We're going to the open house at the Nature Center," Donna said.

"We want to try and lose Mickey on the night sensory course," Larry added.

"Good!" Mary Louise laughed. "Sounds like fun, and should give us a quiet night here then."

CHAPTER FIFTEEN
MONDAY EVENING

A fair-sized crowd milled around the high-ropes course as Sara, the young woman they had met that morning, described the procedures and pointed out the various obstacles forty feet above their heads. Necks craned up at the tall poles, each with a small platform and connected to other poles by one or more cables, rope ladder-type bridges, or timbers. Three eighth-grade students who were currently staying at the center demonstrated the crossings. Each was hooked to the belay cable above his or her head with a safety strap.

Frannie's palms grew sweaty just watching them. She couldn't imagine that Ben and Nancy had done this the other day, not once but twice. Sara finished her presentation and asked for questions.

"Does anyone ever freeze up there?" Frannie said, knowing full well that she would. If someone forced her up there at gunpoint, because there would be no other way she would do it.

Sara rolled her eyes. "Oh, yeah. Not too often, but it happens."

"What do you do then?"

"One of us has to go up and talk them down."

Frannie shuddered. Her fear of heights was such that she couldn't even envision standing on one of the relatively stable platforms forty feet in the air, let alone negotiating a swaying cable, safety strap or not.

A man asked about the type and size of cable required and Frannie tuned out at the numbers and specifications. She scanned the course and the surrounding woods. Daylight persisted in the open area of the course but the woods were falling into shadows as the sun descended. Down in a ravine to the left, she thought she saw movement. Glimpses of a dark figure, apparently all in black, between the trees were so brief that she couldn't be sure she saw anything. Maybe just branches moving in the gentle breeze. It brought to mind movies with mercenaries or special ops troops. Why did she think that—was he carrying a gun?

She kept watching the direction she thought the figure was headed but couldn't see anything else. The crowd started to move through the course, still looking up at the suspended figures. Frannie was afraid to look up while she walked, so she stopped to crane her neck up at the first station. And was promptly run into from behind.

"Oof!" said Donna. "Sorry, I was looking up. Did I hurt you?"

Frannie shook her head. "I'm fine. That's why I stopped; I was afraid if I walked and looked up at the same time, I'd end up flat on my face."

They stood by the pole and let the others surge around them. Donna also insisted she could never try the high ropes.

"Rob wants to. Does Larry?"

"He hasn't mentioned it." She glanced back at the woods.

"What are you looking for?" Donna said.

"Nothing. I think my imagination is getting the best of me. I thought I saw something." She pointed in the general direction.

Donna scrutinized the area, none too subtly. Frannie nudged her. "We're getting left behind." They followed the crowd to the last platform, where participants descended to the ground via a zip line. Frannie could feel the exhilaration of the kids coming down the line and wished she wasn't so squeamish about heights.

They chattered on about the course while walking up the hill to the archery range. Frannie had always wanted to try archery but knew her side would not take it at this time. The rest of the group lined up to take their turns, so Frannie found a bench to the side where she could watch. Unfortunately, Deborah McCabe already occupied one end. Frannie sat at the other end and focused on the shooters to offset the chilly silence.

Finally, she steeled herself, turned, and said, "How long have you worked here, Ms. McCabe?"

Deborah looked at her in surprise. "Uh, six years, I guess." She narrowed her eyes. "Why?"

"Just wondering. Seems like it would be a fascinating place to work."

Deborah lowered her shoulders slightly and sat back. "It is. I especially like working with the corporate clients."

Fewer riffraff like us, Frannie thought. But she said, "How long do those programs usually last?"

"From a few days to a week. We focus on team building skills; they're very popular."

Silence again. Frannie watched Larry and Nancy try their hand with the bow; then was amazed at Mickey's obvious skill at the sport.

"Wow. Mickey never fails to surprise us, even after all these years," she commented, half to herself.

Deborah just looked at her with raised eyebrows.

"He's my brother-in-law," Frannie explained. "In the forty years I've known him, I had no idea he did archery."

"You aren't going to try it?"

Frannie then had to explain her fall in the canoe, no doubt confirming Deborah's view of her as an incompetent, meddling klutz.

"That's too bad," Deborah said, but not convincingly. "You might be able to do the night sensory course, but I wouldn't try the obstacle course if I were you."

"Right." Then Frannie had a thought. "Are there any activities where people dress all in black and, like maybe, track each other through the woods?"

Now she knew Deborah definitely thought she had lost her marbles. "Why would we have that?"

"I don't know. When we were watching the high ropes course, I thought I saw someone in the trees. But it was hard to see so I wasn't sure...I almost had the impression that he—or she—was carrying some kind of military weapon." Now I've done it, she thought. She'll slip out her phone and call the funny farm.

But Deborah's reaction was unexpected. She paled, opened her mouth once and closed it, and finally stammered, "I'm sure...it was no such thing. It might have been...a staff member cutting through who just happened to be dressed in dark clothes...um...maybe carrying equipment needed somewhere..."

"You're probably right. The eyes can play tricks on you when you get to be my age."

Instead of agreeing, as Frannie expected, Deborah looked her watch and jumped up. "I need to help at one of the other sites. Better run." She took off at a fast walk down a path through the trees.

Frannie sat dumbfounded. That woman was strung so tight, she ought to hum like one of the bow strings. She was still mulling it over, when her group approached.

"Did you see Mickey shoot? He's been holding out on us," Nancy said.

"I was Robin Hood in an earlier life," Mickey said.

"You were more likely the court jester," Larry said.

"Not to interrupt this scintillating conversation, but it's about time for the night sensory course to start," Ben reminded them.

After consulting the map, they decided the best way was the trail that Deborah McCabe had taken a short time before. Larry had a flashlight to guide Frannie down the shadowy path.

The night sensory course started at the bottom of a ravine. A small three-sided shed with a bench provided an area where participants could wait without being able to see the course.

Since Frannie hadn't been able to participate in any of the other activities, the group urged her to go first. Larry would be her partner. A middle-aged man, balding but fit, organized the participants and gave them directions. Larry tied the blindfold on Frannie and guided her hand to the rope at the start of the course.

"You won't let me grab any snakes or anything, will you?" She raised her face to the trees, and when Larry's promise came from behind her, turned and said, "Oops. There you are."

He turned her around and headed her up the slope. Feeling her way along the rope, she came to a tree trunk.

"What kind is it?" Larry asked.

"Well, how would I—oh!" She felt pieces of curling bark lifting away from the trunk. "Is it a birch?"

"Correct. Stand still a minute and listen." She did.

"I think I hear a tree frog."

"You do. Okay, the rope goes down here."

She felt it inclining toward the ground. Following it down, she could feel a log. The rope ran along the top of the log.

"Do I have to crawl?"

"Either that, or duck-walk."

She tried that but decided crawling was her only option. She got down on all fours and picked her way along the log.

"They wouldn't put this where there was poison ivy, would they?"

"No, they wouldn't," came her husband's disembodied voice above her. At the end of the log, the rope inclined up again, so she got to her feet with Larry's help. The rope turned around a large stump.

"Stump," she said.

"Good one. How'd you figure that out?"

"Shut up and don't make fun."

The course continued uphill from tree to tree. She found herself listening more and more carefully for clues to her surroundings.

"Mr. Shoemaker?" A voice came from behind them — the man running the course. "There's someone here with a message from the sheriff."

Larry hesitated. "Okay. Can you wait here with my wife while I go see what it is?"

"I should go back in case others come…"

"That's fine, Larry. I'll just stay right here and not move. I can practice listening," Frannie said.

"You're sure? You could take your blindfold off…"

"No, that would spoil it. If the sheriff wants you to go somewhere, have someone come tell me and I'll take my blindfold off then and quit."

She heard them go back down the trail and clung to the rope with her right hand. At first she held her body rigid until she realized that she would be more comfortable if she shifted her feet and relaxed. There was a little soughing wind in the trees and the tree frogs, but no song birds at this time of day. An owl hooted, startling her, and then a flutter somewhere above her head—the owl? Or, her worst fear, a bat? She shifted again to keep from locking her knees and scuffed some sticks. Footsteps again—good, Larry coming back, so silly to allow this fear to grow, and she opened her mouth to call to him when a hard gloved hand clamped over it and another hand grabbed lower at her throat pulling her back against her attacker. Her tender ribs screamed in pain and she grabbed at the hand around her throat with her left hand, urgently clinging to the rope with her right as if it were a lifeline. In desperation, she clamped down with her teeth on the hand covering her open mouth, getting just a couple of fingers, and bit as hard as she could.

A yelp in her ear and a slight release, enough that she could turn her head and scream. "Larry!"

Her assailant tried to drag her off the path but still she clung to the rope. Now there were footsteps running back up the path toward her. It encouraged her to hang on even tighter. The attacker grunted and dropped her, crashing off through the brush on the side of the trail. She had been pulling so hard on the rope that when he let go of her, her body careened sideways over the rope, starting to somersault. Not again. But Larry was there, catching her, and helping her get upright.

Still blindfolded, she pointed to the left. Her voice squeaked. "He went…"

"Don't say 'thataway,' please." He let her go and removed the blindfold. She heard a great deal of thrashing 'thataway' and looked up at her husband, relieved but perplexed.

"Ben and the guide went after him," Larry explained. "Let's get back down to the others. That can't have been good for your side."

She tried to take a deep breath but thought better of it. "I'm jinxed," was all she could say.

More careful baby steps down the path. This was getting old. They reached the level area near the beginning.

She said to Larry, "What was the message?"

"It was a set-up. As soon as the guide left to come get me, the 'messenger' took off. Nancy and Donna got glimpses of him but can't describe him very well."

She stopped in the path and turned around to face him. "You mean, they were after *me*? *Why*?"

"Well, Frannie, people notice when you become involved in these things. You're making yourself a target..."

She held up her hands. "Okay, okay. Did they call the sheriff?"

"Couldn't get a signal down here. Nancy went up the hill to call. Was this guy armed?"

"I didn't see anything—" and realized that was a stupid thing to say since she was blindfolded. "I mean, he had one hand on my mouth and one on my throat, so he couldn't have been holding a gun."

They had just reached the others when more crashing off to their right signaled the emergence of Ben and the guide from the woods with Frannie's attacker struggling between them. When she got a look at his face, there was no recognition. A young man, late teens or early twenties, with freckles and a nest of reddish-blonde hair projecting at all angles, a perfect candidate for a Disney movie except for his surly expression.

The guide looked a little winded but none the worse for wear. "Did somebody call the sheriff?"

"Nancy went back to the archery range to try and get a signal. About ten minutes ago," Mickey said.

"Do you know this kid?" Larry asked the guide.

"I've seen him around but don't know his name. He won't say anything."

"Don't have to say anything," the kid muttered. His voice was rather high and thin.

"Let's get him back up to the archery range," said the guide, looking to Ben for help. "If the sheriff isn't there, we can use him for a target."

The kid was startled out of his scowl for a few seconds, but quickly went back into his tough-guy pose. Larry fell in behind Ben and the guide as they marched the kid up the path.

Jane Ann had come over to Frannie's side. "Are you all right? What did he do?"

"I'm okay. He just grabbed me but fortunately I had my mouth open and was able to bite him—he took his hand away just enough that I could scream."

Jane Ann chuckled. "And our husbands think we should keep our mouths shut! Where would you be then?"

Frannie shuddered. She didn't want to think about it. She made it back to the range with the group, by convincing herself that she had to make it because that was the only way she would see her bed again.

Nancy waited for them and they stood in a little group apart from Ben, Larry, the guide, and the prisoner. Donna had been jabbering all the way up the hill, but Frannie hadn't been listening.

Now she said, " Frannie, you poor thing! You'd better stay in bed tomorrow!"

"Talked me into it," Frannie said.

Headlights pulled into the parking lot. Mary Sorenson jumped out of her car and beelined for the men holding the kid.

"Well, Kyle Robertson. You can't seem to stay out of trouble. This is a little more serious than shoplifting. Assault? What's the matter with you?"

CHAPTER SIXTEEN

LATE MONDAY NIGHT

"I want to call my attorney," Kyle Robertson muttered.

Sorenson cocked her head and raised her eyebrows. "You have an attorney? I hope you keep him or her on retainer, because you are going to need one. Turn around."

She handcuffed him and put him in the back seat of the patrol car, closed the door, then turned back to the group. "So what happened?"

Frannie and Larry told the story with a few additions from the others.

"And you've never seen Kyle before?" the sheriff asked Frannie.

"No, I'm sure not."

"This is really peculiar. He must think you're a threat for some reason, the way this was set up."

Frannie told Sorenson about the figure she had seen in the trees earlier.

"Did he see you watching him?"

"I don't think so. It was so quick that I wasn't even sure what I had seen."

"He probably doesn't know that."

175

Donna inserted herself between Frannie and the sheriff. "Do you think they're connected to the meth lab? Or the murders? Or both?"

"But Barb saw a woman leave the meth lab trailer," Jane Ann said.

"I don't know that Kyle and his friend are connected to either. They may have been up to something else tonight and think your friend saw too much."

While they bandied around theories, Frannie thought about Deborah McCabe's strange reaction to Frannie's questions about the dark figure. She couldn't imagine the woman, unpleasant as she was, being mixed up with the drug trade or the murders, and hated to make wild accusations.

"I wanted to stop by and talk to you tonight anyway," Sorenson said. "The techs found some interesting things on Valerie's phone. Are you going to be up for a while?"

Frannie looked at her watch. Only 8:45. "Sure," she said.

Sorenson walked around toward the driver's side of her car. "I'll take him in," she said over the roof of the car, "and then I'll be back. Will you be here or at the campground?"

Frannie looked at the others. "I'm ready to go back. How about you guys?"

"Oh, yeah," Mickey said. "I'm too old for this stuff."

"Frannie got attacked, and Ben helped catch him, and *you're* the one who's exhausted?" Larry chided him.

Frannie sighed and looked back at Sorenson. "We'll separate these two and go back to the campground."

"Good," Sorenson said. "I think I'll let this guy cool his heels a little bit before I question him so I won't be long. I want your take on this."

They speculated on the way back to the campground about what Sorenson might have found, and continued their conjectures around the fire. They didn't have long to wait. The sheriff's car pulled up to their site about twenty minutes after they did.

Rob got her a chair and she looked around at the group. "You do understand that you need to keep this in your group."

They all agreed, and Sorenson continued. "We found a cell on the strangled woman, and assuming that she had her own phone, that was Valerie." She looked at Frannie. "In that case, you were right in your identification of them. The techs were able to find a deleted message from Richard Ellis-Reynolds arranging a meeting at 9:30 that morning at the power plant and instructing Valerie to wear her necklace."

Frannie said, "Wow. That means...Valerie told me the night before that Virginia had posed as her in order to break it off with Richard. She must have been trying to do it again!"

Sorenson nodded.

"But if Valerie had her own phone, how did Virginia see the message?" said Jane Ann.

"We don't know that. We're assuming that she saw it before either of them left their camper that morning and deleted it. It would explain why one hiked to the plant and one drove. Neither of them knew the other was going there."

"But how did Valerie find out about the meeting if Virginia saw it first and deleted it?" Ben asked.

Mary Sorenson gave them a smug smile. "There was also a call to Richard's phone from Valerie's about 9:00."

Frannie sat back in her chair. "If nothing else, it certainly puts the lie to Richard's statement that he hardly knew Valerie."

"What if it was Virginia with Valerie's phone?" Mickey said.

"That's possible," Sorenson admitted. "But everything except the necklace points to the woman who was knocked into the machinery as Virginia. We should get confirmation of that with the fingerprints tomorrow. We are certain that she died first. Assuming that is Virginia, Valerie's arm was thrown over Virginia's legs. And, based on what you say, the necklace would be explained if she was posing as Valerie."

"*What a tangled web we weave...*" Mickey quoted.

"Seems like the key is that camera case. Val and Virginia *must* have taken pictures that got them killed."

Mary Sorenson nodded. "It's the damnedest thing I ever saw. Two of my deputies are picking up Richard now for questioning so I'd better be getting back." She stood and put her hands in her pockets. "Thank you for your help. You guys are good. But of course that doesn't mean I want you actively involved. Stay safe." She turned and walked to her car.

"Could there be any connection between Richard and the guys who set up the attack on you?" Jane Ann said to Frannie.

"Who knows? We ran into the same question at Bat Cave and Bluffs. How could any of these people from all different places be connected to each other?" She paused and looked at the others. "When you guys were on the archery range, I mentioned to Deborah McCabe that I thought I had seen someone dressed in dark clothes going through the woods earlier. I thought maybe it was another exercise they had going on tonight. She seemed to be very shocked and alarmed and jumped up and hurried down that path we took to the night sensory course."

"Did you tell Mary Sorenson any of that?" Larry asked.

"No—well, I told her about seeing someone in the woods, but not about McCabe's reaction. I hate to throw accusations around... But we saw her this morning arguing with Dale Dubrak. I wonder if he's buddies with the guys who attacked me."

Larry shook his head. "Frannie, she needs to know all this stuff. You can't keep anything back, thinking you're going to go off investigating on your own."

His accusation made her mad. "I'm not planning any investigating! I am just not sure how to interpret Deborah McCabe's reaction and I don't want to accuse her just because I don't like her personally."

Larry held up his hands but lowered his voice. "I know. But I think Sorenson is pretty level-headed and won't throw McCabe in the brig without more foundation than that. How about if we call her in the morning and you tell her about it? Maybe she'll fill us in on what she finds out from that Kyle kid and Richard tonight."

Frannie relaxed and smiled. "You sneak. You want to solve this as bad as I do."

"Maybe."

Later, laying in bed, she mulled over the characters in this drama and tried to see connections. Maybe there were several things going on that weren't connected—just coming to light because of the murder investigation? She got out of bed and found her sweatshirt.

"Can't sleep?"

"No."

"Me either." Larry sat up and swung his legs out of the bed.

"Do you want me to start the coffee?"

He looked over his shoulder at her to see if she was serious. "Good Lord, no."

So he fixed them mugs of herbal tea while she turned on a small lamp over the dinette and found a notebook in a cubby. They sat facing each other, hands wrapped around their steaming mugs. The warmth felt good in the late night chill. She suspected she had the beginnings of arthritis in her hands. Her mother had suffered with it for many years.

"What's the notebook for?" Larry said.

"Organizing my thoughts—*our* thoughts."

With a pencil, she started a word web with two circles in the center containing the twins names.

"I'm trying to work out some of the connections in this situation. I thought maybe if I could draw it out it would make more sense."

"Good luck with that," he said wryly, but watched what she was doing with interest.

She drew circles around the outside for the names of the major players. "Richard. A couple of possibilities." She drew a line from Richard's circle to Val's and wrote 'tired of her? Interfered w/ other romance?' and then a line to Virginia with 'obstacle to romance with Val?' on it.

Larry said, "Maybe he thought Virginia was Val because of the necklace, and killed her thinking he was getting rid of Val." She added that to the web.

"I feel certain that, because of the timing, the murderer had to have known about and escaped through the tunnel. Richard has been here several times and also may have had a relative who knew about the tunnel in the late twenties. I found a Reynolds from Chicago on the 'Net who was involved in bootlegging in the late twenties. He knew at least one of the twins was at the power plant."

"Because he set it up," Larry pointed out.

She looked at him and chewed her lip. "You're right. But why kill both? If you are right about his motive to kill Val, he had no reason to get rid of Virginia and vice-versa. Eliminate a witness?"

She moved on. Dale Dubrak went in the next circle clockwise. "We know a little about Richard and the twins but nothing about whether Dale had even seen them. The best I can do is 'training' and 'attitude.' Excellent bases for suspicion. Maybe the twins had compromising pictures of him."

"Training?" Larry said.

"He mentioned he was 'training' when we gave him a ride but wouldn't say for what. Kind of odd. I assume he knows about the tunnel since he is from the area. He has a temper—we saw that at the tavern."

She wrote 'Kyle Robertson' in the next circle. "I have no idea what his motive might be for the murders, or for that matter, for assaulting me." She drew a line from Kyle's circle to Dale's with a question mark. "It shouldn't be too hard to find out if they are friends or at least know each other." Another circle with a question mark represented the 'messenger' who undoubtedly knew Kyle, but maybe also Dale. It seemed like any motive these young men might have would involve photos that the twins had inadvertently taken of them doing something illegal.

"Don't forget the meth lab folks," Larry said.

She complied but said, "We have no idea whether the twins had any knowledge of this lab or connections with the people who ran it."

"We don't know much about any of these suspects," Larry said.

"True." She tried unsuccessfully to stifle a huge yawn.

He raised his eyebrows. "You should be exhausted."

"I am," she admitted. "Wait—one more." She added another circle and wrote 'Claire' in it.

"Who's Claire?"

"Richard's squeeze that I met at the diner. *She* might have motive if she felt Richard was really interested in Val."

"Not sure how strong Richard and Claire's motives were," Larry said. "Richard lived in Chicago; the twins in the Cities. You said their paths hadn't crossed in four years. There's no reason they should again. But if the twins had pictures that would expose another suspect's illegal activity, it would be a much more compelling motive to get rid of them."

"You're right. We'll take a fresh look in the morning. Take me to bed before I have to crawl there."

CHAPTER SEVENTEEN
EARLY TUESDAY MORNING

Frannie slept well, finally, but woke early the next morning. Once the dog chores were done and the coffee made, she sat under the trailer awning, watching the morning unfold, her notebook in her lap.

It was a glorious morning. Her side felt better in spite of her antics the night before. They would be returning home the next day, so she thought about what she would like to do today and heard the putter of Mary Louise's golf cart.

The hostess's flaming red curls caught glints of the morning sun as she bounced up the slight grade towards Frannie's chair.

"Hey!" Mary Louise sported tight jeans and an ice blue t-shirt with a glittery design proclaiming *Girls Just Wanna Have Fun.*

"You are looking a little perkier, young lady!" she said, settling herself in a nearby chair.

Frannie laughed.

"What?" Mary Louise looked offended. "You are!"

"Thank you—I do feel much better. I'm just laughing because I must be twenty years older than you at least.

No one has called me 'young lady' since one of my dad's old war buddies when I was about twelve."

Mary Louise waved her off. "Heck, it's all in your mind. And *you* have a young mind."

Frannie smiled. "Thank you again. Would you like some coffee?" She nodded toward the coffee pot.

"No, not me. Can you imagine me on caffeine?"

"I see what you mean. So why are you out and about so early?"

"Just checking to see what areas need to be mowed before the next weekend and saw you out here."

"I love early mornings," Frannie said. "Always have. I think when my kids were little, it was the only time I had to myself."

Mary Louise nodded with understanding. She lowered her voice a few decibels. "You know, I think you're right about that Ellis-Reynolds guy being a ladies' man. I've seen that dark-haired chick around there a couple of times, but guess who he was flirting with last night?"

Frannie waited, thinking the question was rhetorical. When no enlightenment was forthcoming, she said, "Who?"

"Jonie." She sat smugly while Frannie's jaw dropped.

"Are you kidding me? I can't think of anyone less like Claire than Jonie."

"Who's Claire?"

"The dark-haired chick," Frannie smiled. "So what was he doing with Jonie? I don't need details...just general terms."

"Well, I couldn't hear everything but she started chatting with him as she walked by and I did hear him say he might know someone to help her career. That's all it takes with Jonie. She's in love." Mary Louise rolled her eyes.

"And in for a big disappointment, I imagine. I can't believe he'd follow through on that offer. But I'm biased. I think he's pretty sleazy."

"He promised to come hear her sing tonight at Farrell's. Jim and I may need to take that in."

Frannie had a hard time picturing Richard in the down-at-its-heels bar, but who knew? Maybe it would be worth a return trip.

Jane Ann came out of her camper with a steaming mug. "Good morning!"

"And a beautiful one it is," Mary Louise replied. "'Specially brought to you by River Bend for your pleasure."

"Thank you," Jane Ann said, pulling a chair near them. "You two look like the proverbial cats that ate the canary. What's up?"

Frannie shared the update on Jonie and Richard. Jane Ann raised her eyebrows and said, "Wow. Jonie? Talk about the odd couple."

They visited a few more minutes and Mary Louise excused herself to get back to her campground duties. One by one, members of their group emerged in various states of dress and wakefulness. By the time they had prepared breakfast and cleared it away, the sheriff's car approached their conclave.

"Well?" Frannie prodded, when Mary had joined their circle. "How did the interrogations go last night?"

"Interesting," Sorenson said. "Your friend Richard admitted that he did know Valerie Peete and that he went to the power plant that morning."

"And? Did he confess?"

"No, no, he's totally innocent—according to him. He says when he got there, early by the way, Valerie was the only one there. At least he thought it was Valerie because of the necklace. It had to have been Virginia. Anyway, she told him she never wanted to see him again and that was that. He left and knows nothing more about it."

Frannie compressed her lips. "I don't want to believe him. But," she paused a minute and looked out at the trees, "what if he's telling the truth? The real Valerie arrives and finds out what happened and knocks her sister into the machinery in a fit of rage?"

"Then who killed Valerie?" Mickey asked.

"Could she have strangled herself in remorse?" Nancy asked the sheriff.

"I've done a little research on that. It is possible but not common," the sheriff said.

"There's still the missing camera bag. If it was a murder-suicide, what happened to it?"

"Exactly. There's the rub," said Sorenson. "That's a big reason I don't think that's what happened."

"What about Kyle Robertson?" Frannie said. "Did you find out why he targeted me?"

Sorenson shifted in her chair and shook her head. "He's still not talking. He's being charged with assault."

"Do you know if he is friends with Dale Dubrak?"

"As a matter of fact he is. Dale is lucky he hasn't gotten in trouble with Kyle several times. Why?"

Frannie recounted her dealings with Dale, the argument they had observed with Deborah McCabe, and McCabe's reaction to Frannie's questions about the dark figure in the trees.

Sorenson sighed. "Here's what I think. When we searched Kyle, we found a pamphlet on him called *44 Ways to Support Jihad.* It has become pretty widely known and is popular with loners who are terrorist wannabes."

"Terrorists?" Donna sat forward, vocalizing the shock they all felt.

"We have found no connection with anyone or any groups outside. But this pamphlet can be downloaded off the internet. Kyle had printed it off his home computer. The pages about physical fitness and arms training are the only ones that show any signs of use. He doesn't appear to have spent much time on the instructions for prayer and so on. But I think he, his messenger mate, and possibly Dubrak seem to have been trying to prepare themselves physically to join a terrorist group. With the information you've given me this morning, I'm wondering if Kyle and his buddies haven't been using the Nature Center for their physical fitness regimen and also if Deborah McCabe isn't helping them."

"Other than the literature," Larry said, "is there anything else to indicate that?"

"Not anything concrete," Mary got up and refilled her coffee mug. "And I'm doing a little amateur profiling here. But Dale and Kyle have been mavericks since they were about twelve. Except for each other, they don't have a lot of friends. It would explain what you thought you saw in the trees — them practicing some kind of maneuvers, real or imaginary. And if for some unknown reason Deb is helping them, she would be angry they were doing this during the open house."

"But why me?" Frannie said. "All I did was ask Dale what he was training for and told Deborah I thought I saw someone in the trees. I don't *know* anything."

Sorenson leaned forward. "It doesn't matter what you know. It matters what they *think* you know or think you *might* know." Her brown curls bounced as she shook her head. "They — or at least Kyle and Dale — aren't exactly grounded in reality."

"What do you know about Deborah McCabe?" Nancy asked. "Is she from around here?"

"Not originally," said the sheriff. "She came here in high school — junior or senior year, I think — to live with an aunt and uncle. Her parents were killed in a car accident. She went to community college around here and came back to work at the Center, but she's never been the most cheerful sort. I don't know that she has any friends — but it's pretty tough for any kid to change schools at that stage."

"Getting back to Richard the Sleaze," Frannie said, "Mary Louise told me this morning that last night he apparently made promises to Jonie about helping her career. Did you find out anything from him about his background?"

"That's interesting that he seems to have moved on so quickly. Didn't learn much—just that he's in finance and that he and his 'girlfriend,' Claire Devon, have been coming here for several years. I checked this Claire's background and she's a Chicago heiress, but they have no marriage plans, he says."

"What about the people with the meth lab?" Jane Ann said.

"Right. We have their names...those prints were in the system. Two men and a woman who have been arrested for drugs before. We have an APB out for them. They haven't been picked up yet so we don't know much. But it's certainly possible that trailer caught the twins' eye and that they could have taken pictures of it—maybe with someone coming out or looking out a window or something. A definite motive for murder. Well, time to move on." Sorenson turned to Frannie. "If you think of anything else regarding those boys, please let me know right away."

"Will do."

As the sheriff drove away, Larry said, "What's on the schedule for today?"

"We wanted to ride toward Newton," Nancy said. "Ben said there is a little farm along the river. All of the buildings are painted purple and the women who own it sell hand-knitted socks and hats."

"The Purple Goat Farm," Donna said, sitting forward. "I forgot about that place. I wanna go too." Only shopping could entice Donna on a long bike ride.

"We didn't see any purple goats," Rob said.

"The goats aren't purple, silly," Donna said. "They raise angora goats. I don't remember what the name of the place really is but that's what we called it. Because the buildings are purple. Remember, Jane Ann? We went there several years ago."

"Yup, and I took Frannie there the next time we were up here." Jane Ann looked at Frannie. "Are you up for it?"

Frannie hesitated a minute. "Much as I would love to, I think not. Fear of falling. Think I'll read this morning and do a little walking."

After she convinced them again that she was fine by herself, and making them promise not to have pie without her, the rest of the group mounted their bikes and wove and tottered out of the campground.

Frannie read awhile, but found her concentration constantly interrupted by thoughts of the twins' murders. This intrusion of violence seemed like a collision of universes. The intersection of criminal events with her mundane, very average life was just surreal. Until the murder they had encountered at Bat Cave State Park several months before, she had never in her whole life seen anyone brandish a gun in any kind of threatening way. She thought back over her brief visit with Valerie and later both twins. Val's biggest concern appeared to be her romance with Richard. She acknowledged to herself that the conversation around the fire was very superficial, yet she felt sure neither twin exhibited any nervousness or sign that they were under threat of danger.

She needed a stretch so she grabbed a walking stick from the trailer and, after deciding that Cuba looked too comfortable curled up in the shade, started along the campground road. Along the way, she detoured to check out the wildlife at the river's edge and admire a bald eagle circling above the cliffs.

Her wanderings took her to the west end of the campground, not entirely accidentally. She was curious about the path leading up to the Nature Center and whether the power plant was still taped off by the sheriff's department.

She saw no signs of activity around the Dubraks' old trailer so decided to try the path. It was an uphill climb but quite gradual.

As she trudged up the path, she noticed a few spring wildflowers nestled among the understory trees. The sun picked out clusters of leaves to highlight gold in the dark woods. A few birds chirped and the air had a musty spring scent—a combination of new growth and freshly turned dirt. She rounded a turn in the path and stopped short at the site of a figure silhouetted and coming toward her.

It was Deborah McCabe. McCabe's eyes widened in surprise. She stepped off the path to let Frannie pass, looking down at the ground, and then hurried on toward the campground. Frannie turned and watched her, wondering if she was looking for Dale Dubrak. Frannie had never seen her near the trailer, but there weren't a lot of other people left camping now that it was midweek.

Obviously, McCabe wasn't coming to visit Frannie and her friends.

Still puzzling over Deborah's visit to the campground, she almost missed the trail to the power plant. Picking her way slowly through the protruding roots and overgrowth, she reached the landing in front of the gaping door. There was no crime scene tape, but she had no desire to go in, the memory of the women's bodies feeling like a hole in her stomach.

Edging her way along the front of the building, she peeked around the corner. Grass on the steep hillside was trampled and branches broken; she assumed this was the result of the investigation, but maybe others had been exploring there as well, possibly looking for the missing camera bag. Working back to the other front corner, she saw that the view along the other side was pretty much the same.

She sat on a rock outcropping facing the door to rest a moment. If the killer wanted to get rid of the camera bag, the easiest thing would have been to pitch it out one of the windows on the river side of the building. She wondered if the sheriff's people had checked the river.

A crack from the trees to her right startled her and made her stomach flip again. Her palms were damp as she turned and peered into the tangled growth. She would have go that way to get back to the main path, so she sat very still listening. No further sounds other than the breeze rustling the trees.

After several minutes, she got to her feet, and with the help of the walking stick, made her way back up the path. About halfway up, another noise stopped her. Nearer this time. The back of her neck prickled and she had just decided she'd better get back to the main path as quickly as she could when a large furry shape scurried across the trail ahead of her.

A raccoon. She laughed in relief and realized how jumpy this place made her, even in mid-morning on a sunny day. Picking up the pace, she soon reached the main path and headed back down toward the campground.

She concentrated on her footing and heard rather than saw someone step out of the trees in front of her. Deborah McCabe faced her again from just a couple of feet away. Frannie glanced back over her shoulder. No sign of anyone else around them, friend or foe.

"Hi," she said, her voice only cracking a little. How could a morning walk turn into such a scary event?

"Um...sorry if I startled you," Deborah said, glancing from Frannie to the trees and back again..

"Well, yes, you did," Frannie said. "Did you want something?"

Deborah tried to keep her all-business demeanor. "Yes." She looked to the other side into the trees. Frannie waited. What was this woman up to now? She slipped one hand in the pocket where she kept her phone and gripped her walking stick tighter with the other.

"I just...well, I wanted to apologize...you know, for what you went through last night."

Frannie frowned. "Apologize?"

"Well, you see, I sort of made allowances that I shouldn't have. I mean, Dale and Kyle said they wanted to practice some training that they were taking...they didn't say what but nobody gives them much of a break and it's hard to be an outsider here..."

To Frannie's surprise, tears welled up in Deborah's eyes and she began blinking rapidly.

"So I told them I would help them." Deborah swallowed and continued. "I had *no* idea what their plans were...the sheriff questioned me this morning and told me about the terrorist literature they had." She took a deep breath and composed herself. "I had *no* idea."

"Deborah, do you think they could have been involved in, you know, what happened to those two women?"

"What? *No*, definitely not! I walked down here that morning and Dale was still in bed."

"You did? Before we saw you at the center?"

"Of course. I don't start work until 9:00."

Frannie thought a moment. "Did you see anyone else on this path."

Deborah looked at her, eyes wide, as she realized the significance of the question. "Just that guy from Chicago. The one who's been trying to make time with like half the women here." The bitter tone told Frannie that Deborah was in the other half.

"Well, do you know why the boys attacked *me*?" Frannie said. "I mean it was obviously planned."

"I think you asked too many questions. You do, you know." Deborah had regained her haughty, defensive posture.

"I suppose I do," Frannie admitted, "but I'm just curious about people. Well, thank you for telling me."

Deborah gave a curt nod, and stepped back off the path so that Frannie could continue down the hill.

After a few steps, Frannie looked back. Deborah briskly headed up the hill, her back ramrod straight.

Had she been attracted to Kyle and Dale because of being a loner herself? It appeared she was regretting her involvement, and Frannie was sure the apology was extremely difficult for her. As she picked her way down the hill with the aid of her stick, she was taken suddenly back to being an outsider herself, as a new junior high teacher in their present home of Perfection Falls. She met Larry at the local roller skating rink; he was one of the local skating hotshots and dazzled her with his prowess on the floor. Most of his relatives and childhood friends still lived in the same town, and she remembered the feeling of rootlessness—of having no identity or past when she was around them. In some ways it seemed like yesterday; in others like it was someone else's experience. Time and memory were very strange.

CHAPTER EIGHTEEN
LATE TUESDAY MORNING

Almost back to her campsite, Frannie caught up with Jonie Rump, gamely tottering along in purple spike heels. Her lavender top was again off-the-shoulder, but in deference to the morning hour, she wore jeans. Formfitting jeans that stopped mid-calf and were studded with rhinestone designs on the back pockets, but jeans nonetheless.

Jonie heard her coming and turned back, her face breaking into a wide smile. However, her lavender eyelids appeared puffy and a couple of telltale streaks of mascara leaked from her eyes.

"Hey!"

"Beautiful morning," Frannie said, returning the smile.

"Been fer a walk?"

"I have." They strolled along together like old friends, although Jonie's stroll was more lurching, and Frannie was tempted to offer her the walking stick. "And you?"

"I had to talk to Mel." Jonie paused, took a deep breath and stared straight ahead. Frannie waited and finally she continued. "I'm afraid he's kinda sweet on me —," she lowered her eyelids coyly, "and I thought I should set 'im straight, as gently as I could, acourse." She glanced at Frannie for approval.

"Of course," Frannie agreed. "I take it the feeling wasn't mutual?"

"Wha—? Oh, yeah, I see what ya mean. Well, he's been a friend a long time, but not like that. I don't think he understood, though, and now that I'll probly be leavin'..." Frannie noticed again that Jonie seemed to slip in and out of her version of a Southern drawl much easier than it would be to slip out of those jeans.

"Leaving? Are you moving, or going on a trip?" They had come to Frannie's campsite road so she stopped and faced Jonie.

"It's kind of a secret—do y'all have time for a little visit?"

"Sure," Frannie said. "My friends are all off biking and I would love a little company. Would you like some coffee?"

"Oh, I'd love some. That is so sweet."

As they continued to the campsite, Jonie asked her about where else they camped and other safe subjects until Frannie had poured her a mug of coffee and refreshed her own. Once seated by the campfire ring, Jonie returned to her secret.

"Y'see," she leaned forward in her lawn chair, even though no one else was around to hear, "I'm finally getting my big break."

"That's wonderful," Frannie said. "What's happened?"

"There's a man camping here who has connections with some *big* people in the music business. He's gonna come hear me sing tonight and get me introduced. By this time next week, I could be performin' in Nashville!" She sat back with a big smile, her breakup with Mel forgotten.

"Sounds great—who is the man?" Frannie asked, pretty sure she already knew the answer.

"His name's Richard Ellis-Reynolds. It's a *hyphenated* name."

Frannie didn't reply right away. How much to say? Especially when she didn't *know* anything for sure. But Jonie was a sweet lady but seemed pretty gullible.

"Um, have you checked him out? I mean, how do you know he has these connections?"

"Check him out? How would I do that? He *seems* on the up and up." Jonie became so disconcerted that she lost her drawl completely.

Frannie sighed. "I'm sure he does, but...I don't know anything for certain but I think he makes promises to women and doesn't intend to carry them out."

"Oh, I think you're very wrong—no disrespect intended." Jonie shook her head. Jonie continued on about the names and studios Richard had said he knew and how one of them would surely come through for her.

"He's gonna loan me what I need to make this work. Could well be my last chance and I'm going to take it." She paused for a breath. "I have an uncle who's pretty well off and he's told me I'm his only heir. But he's pretty healthy, and 'course I don't wish him ill, so Richard said he'd help me out."

Frannie couldn't think of a single fact she could present to refute all that.

"Well, I gotta be goin'. Thanks for the coffee," Jonie got out of her lawn chair and tiptoed toward the road on her spikes.

"Good luck, Jonie!" Frannie called after her. "I hope it all works out for you." And she hoped it did. But she mistrusted Richard's intentions, even though she couldn't imagine what his motive would be in helping Jonie other than good will. She also knew she just plain didn't want to grant Richard the benefit of the doubt.

She had just gotten back into her book when she felt a familiar nuzzle under her right arm. She looked down into Cuba's liquid brown eyes, pleading for a walk. Getting the leash, she thought maybe Richard would be hanging around outside and some discreet pumping would be possible. Right.

Cuba strained at the leash as they ambled along the road, itching to explore empty campsites for food and dog smells. A couple of sites still held RVs, one with a man her age reading a thick paperback while his wife sat at the picnic table perusing the morning paper. They both looked up and nodded and the woman said, "Nice dog."

Frannie nodded her thanks. "She loves to camp."

When she reached the office area, she was disappointed that Richard's site looked deserted and his bike was nowhere to be seen.

She stopped in the office to return a paperback that she had borrowed earlier from Mary Louise. Phun Munki lay curled up fat and sassy on the counter, stretched out on the guest ledger. She raised her head and gave Cuba a hiss, which the dog ignored. Cats were beneath Cuba's dignity.

Mary Louise bustled out from the back office.

"Long time, no see!" she fairly shouted. And then let loose with her unique hoot of laughter.

"Right," Frannie grinned back at her.

"What can I do for you?"

"Just returning a book I borrowed the other day." She laid it on the counter. "I seem to have a lot of time to read this trip."

Mary Louise turned serious. "That's a shame, honey. I'm so sorry about that fall."

Frannie waved her off. "Not your fault. I've been canoeing for forty years, Mary Louise, and I know better than jumping into a canoe without making sure it's floating! Don't think another thing—"

The phone on the counter shrilled an interruption. Mary Louise held up one finger, bracelets jangling, and reached for the phone with the other hand.

"Good morning! River Bend Campground!" For the second time, her wide smile disappeared and a little frown formed between carefully plucked brows. She listened for a minute more and then, "Okay, Sheriff. Anything we can do." She hung up the phone and looked back up at Frannie.

"Sheriff has a warrant to search Mel Dubrak's trailer. They're looking for that camera case and think it might be there."

"Huh!" Frannie said. "On what basis, did she say?"

"Something Kyle let slip in the questioning." She sighed and looked sad. "I know they've been trouble, but I didn't figure those boys for murderers."

"I didn't either," Frannie said, puzzled.

"I feel sorry for Mel. First, suspicion of having a meth lab and now this."

They had only chatted a few minutes longer when the sheriff's car followed by a couple of other patrol cars slowly passed the office windows.

Frannie looked at Mary Louise. "I'm really curious about what they'll find, but I think maybe I'd best wait here until this is over. My husband would be shocked but proud."

Mary Louise clapped her hands, like a child getting ice cream. "Good for you!" She nodded toward a small table in the corner. "I was just playing a little solitaire before you came. How about a game of Doubles?"

"Sure," Frannie said. "Sounds great."

About twenty minutes later when the sheriff's car pulled up again, Mary Louise gathered all of the cards in a pile, knowing that Frannie no longer had any interest in playing. Frannie stood as Sheriff Sorenson walked in the door. The other patrol cars had continued on out of the campground.

The sheriff carried a plastic bag containing a large green shape.

"That's it!" Frannie said.

The sheriff held up the bag by both corners so that Frannie could get a better look. "You're sure?"

Pressed, Frannie backed off a little. "Well, that was definitely the color."

"One of the twins carried something like this that morning when you saw her leave?"

"Yes. Did Kyle admit that they had taken it?"

Mary Sorenson hesitated. "Not exactly. He said if we wanted to know what was going on, we should check Dale's trailer."

"Was it inside?" Mary Louise asked.

"No, underneath the trailer behind some old batteries and tires. No Dale though, he apparently took off. What are you getting at?"

Frannie saw immediately what Mary Louise was thinking. "Anyone could have put it there."

"You think Kyle tried to frame Dale?" the sheriff asked.

"Or someone else did."

"Was that the only suspicious thing you found?" Mary Louise prompted.

"No, we also found more terrorist literature under an old mattress inside."

"What if the camera bag was planted, and Kyle was referring to the stuff you found inside—maybe he just didn't want to go down alone," Frannie said.

The sheriff looked at her and smiled. "I don't *want* this to be complicated."

"Did you find any fingerprints or anything in the twins' camper from the intruders?" Frannie asked.

"Yes, we did. Same ones we found in the seasonal trailer. Where the meth lab was." The sheriff up the bag again. "I think this is going to give us some answers as soon as we check out the memory card, so I need to get back and take care of that. Thanks again."

Frannie and Mary Louise watched her go.

"What are you thinking?" Mary Louise said.

"Seems like it all depends on what's on that camera—assuming they didn't just use that bag for their lunch or extra underwear." She gave a wry smile. "I don't know anything about the people with the meth lab, of course. But if they ransacked the trailer, it seems unlikely that they killed the twins. They may have been looking for incriminating photos and film in the trailer but if one them had done the murdering, they would have had the camera bag."

"Like you said—depends on what is on the camera." Mary Louise wiped down the counter and replaced the ledger.

Frannie thought a minute. "I guess it's possible there was nothing on the camera, so they broke into the trailer to make sure there wasn't anything there. Or if there was incriminating stuff on the camera, that there weren't more copies."

"It does seem like they had the most to lose," Mary Louise said.

"Do you have a busy weekend coming up?" Frannie was tired of trying to wrap her head around all of these suspects.

"Oh, yes, if the weather holds, we'll be busy until fall."

Frannie said her goodbyes and led Cuba back to their campsite. Still no sign of anyone at Richard's site.

The sheriff's findings brought up lots more questions than they answered. Had anyone seen the meth lab people anywhere near the power plant the morning of the murders? Or for that matter any of the other suspects? Then she remembered Deborah had seen Richard, but he had admitted to the sheriff that he had been there and explained his presence, true or not. She was convinced that the murderer had escaped through the old tunnel, but any of the suspects could have known about that. The timing just wouldn't allow for anything else.

It occurred to her now that if whoever stole the camera bag had any tech savvy, he or she would have erased the memory card in the camera by now; so she was eager to hear what the sheriff would find.

At the sound of bikes on the gravel, she looked up to see the rest of her group returning. Donna showed off a pair of hand-knit socks and Mickey shared a funny story about three wild turkeys who ran ahead of the cyclists for about a quarter mile rather than dodge into the brush.

"You can see how turkeys got a reputation for not being too bright," Mickey finished.

Frannie filled the others in on the events of her morning. Larry stood, hands on hips staring in the distance toward the location of the old trailer.

"If the twins had photos of Dale and his friends going through the training courses at the Center, how could that possibly be a threat to them?"

"What do you mean?" Frannie sensed a new perspective.

"Unless they are carrying weapons in the photos, which you would think the twins would have reported, what could they have been doing that would be any different from anyone else using the course?"

"You're right. Well, Mary Louise suggested that the camera bag could have been planted since it wasn't even inside the trailer. It just seems less and less likely that Dale and Kyle were involved in the murders."

Donna had been listening intently. "Don't you just follow the money?"

"What?" Frannie looked at Donna and frowned. "What are you talking about?"

Donna shrugged. "I thought detectives always followed the money."

"I'm not a detective, and I don't pretend to be."

"Oh, I know. I didn't mean that. I just thought they usually look for the money in a case."

It was Frannie's turn to shrug. "I can't think of any connection of money to this case, though."

She mulled over Donna's comments as she fixed some sandwiches for lunch. She and Larry washed up their dishes, and she sat back down at the dinette with her notebook. Looking at the circles, she tried to think of any financial reasons the twins might have been killed. Obviously one of the main motives for operating a meth lab is financial, but the other suspects didn't seem to have money issues that she could see.

The circle with Claire's name caught her eye. She had drawn a line connecting it to Richard's circle. What had Mary Sorenson said about Claire? That she was an heiress, but she and Richard had no plans to marry. She then remembered that the twins had inherited enough money to live comfortably without working full time. But Jonie? How did she fit in? Jonie's and Mary Louise's words came back to her—a rich uncle who was leaving everything to Jonie. She put dollar signs in the twins', Jonie's, and Claire's circles. Maybe Donna had something.

She opened her laptop and did another search on Richard. Scrolling down the list of references, she found the article referring to an investigation into his firm's financial practices earlier in the year. Apparently, it was dropped, because she couldn't find any other mention of the matter.

"Feel like hiking up to the power plant? You said you wanted to go back there," Larry said.

Frannie looked at him skeptically. "What are *you* up to?"

Larry shrugged. "Thought maybe we should see where that tunnel is."

CHAPTER NINETEEN
TUESDAY AFTERNOON

They arrived at the power plant without incident or meeting anyone. Frannie followed Larry down the staircase, one hand on the wall and one on Larry's shoulder.

"Well, the water had to come through the tunnel to the blades of the turbine, and then out the front of the building back into the river," Larry said.

Frannie tried to picture the front of the building as they had passed it on their canoe float.

"Larry! I remember seeing what I thought was a door in the front but it's nowhere near water level. I thought how odd to have a door that high off the water. I bet it's the old outlet."

"Is it on the side? Or in the middle?"

She thought about it. "Definitely on the side." She pointed at the room near where the twins had been found. "I think it's below that window."

Larry took her hand and guided her around the piles of scrap into the smaller room and the window opening. He leaned out the window and looked down.

"Yup. It's down there." He turned around and looked at the back wall.

In the corner a rusted shaft thrust up through the floor. Behind the shaft yawned a gaping hole in the wall.

"We never saw that because we didn't come in here," Larry said. He went behind the shaft and peered into the hole. "There's a ladder down to the tunnel floor, maybe about four feet. I'm going to check it out but you stay here."

"But—."

"No buts. Worst thing you could do for your side." He pulled a small flashlight out of a cargo pocket in his shorts. "I'm just going to see how open it is."

"I don't really want to stay here either."

"I'll stay where I can hear you."

"Okay," she said in a small voice. This stupid injury. She had no patience with being an invalid or being treated like one. She supposed Larry would be in for a rough time, the older she got.

"I could sing," she added.

He grinned. "That might scare some bats out of the tunnel."

"Bats! I forgot about that. I'll stay here."

"I thought you would." He swung a leg over to the second rung of the ladder. Soon he stood on the floor of the tunnel shining his light down.

"A little water still runs through here," he said. "I'm going to check out the part under the power plant and that opening to the river first. I'll just be a minute."

She began reciting some of A. A. Milne's poems that she had read many times to Sam and Sally when they were young, starting with the one about King John's breakfast. She had just gotten to the part where the cow agrees to give milk for the butter for the bread when Larry appeared again at the bottom of the ladder.

"I don't see how anyone could have gotten away that way. It's quite a drop down to the river. I'm going the other way just ten or twenty feet."

He disappeared but she could see the reflection of his light on the walls of the tunnel. She lost her place in the poem, so she started in on "Disobedience" which began with the rhythmic 'James James Morrison Morrison Weatherbee George Dupree' and had only finished the first verse when the light reflections suddenly bounced erratically and she heard scuffling and grunting.

"Larry?" she called out in a panic.

"Call 911!" he yelled back.

"No!" another voice insisted. "I didn't do it!" It sounded like Dale Dubrak but she hadn't heard him talk enough to be sure.

"Hold on, Frannie," Larry said. And then in a lower tone, "If you didn't do it, you *know* something."

"I can't say!" The voice almost squeaked in fear. The light steadied and the shuffling moved back toward the ladder. When they came into view, Larry had Dale's arm twisted behind his back.

"Get up the ladder, and remember, *I* have your gun now."

Frannie pulled back as Dale's head appeared in the opening. He clambered out of the hole ahead of Larry and raised his hands as soon as he got to his feet.

"They're trying to pin those murders on me!" he whined.

"Who is?" Larry asked.

"The sheriff. She's always out to get me and my dad."

"So how did you get the camera bag, if you didn't do it?"

"The what?"

"The sheriff found the camera bag belonging to the murdered women hidden under your dad's trailer."

Dubrak shook his head. "I don't know anything about that. I saw the sheriff's car coming and got out of there. This is a good place to hide."

"Dale," Frannie said gently, playing good cop, "Were you in the tunnel when the women were killed? Did you hear or see something?"

"No!"

"Was it your friend, Kyle?" she pushed.

"No!" he said, more forcefully. "Kyle wouldn't do that!"

"He attacked *me*," she pointed out.

"That was—that was just—" he hung his head and shook it, then looked back up at her. "We just wanted to scare you off. You asked too many questions about what we were doing. He wasn't going to do anything more than that."

Larry got out his phone. "I'm calling the sheriff."

"Please, no," Dale said, his voice muffled. "He threatened me."

"Who? Kyle did?" Larry said.

211

"No, not Kyle." His voice got back the sarcastic edge. "You pigs always pick on anybody who looks different."

Pigs? Frannie hadn't heard that term since the sixties.

"Well, who threatened you? C'mon, Dale, you need to help yourself here," Frannie coaxed.

"This isn't a game," Larry added. "The sheriff will check what's on the camera and if there's pictures that could get you in trouble, you've got a motive to get rid of those women. You'll go away for the rest of your worthless life."

"What did the bag look like?" Dale said.

"Maybe you should tell us—" Larry started to say, but Frannie interrupted.

"Dark green with tan straps."

Larry shot her a warning look.

Dale clamped his mouth shut and shook his head, looking down at the floor.

"Dale," Larry said, holding his phone poised to call.

When Dale looked back up, his left eye twitched and fear clenched his face. "He knows people. He said they'll get me if anything happens to him."

"*Who* said that?"

Again Dale shook his head and lifted his chin. "I know my rights."

Larry smirked as he dialed the sheriff. "But apparently that doesn't give you much respect for the government that protects them."

As he pocketed the phone, he held the gun steady on Dale.

"No reception here. We'll head up to the parking lot, and then you'll have a chance to expound on your rights to the authorities."

Dale had regained some of his confidence. He turned and spat to the side and said, "Pigs." again.

Frannie could see that it took all of her husband's self-control to refrain from backhanding the arrogant young man. Instead, he ordered Dale ahead of him up the stairs and Frannie followed. She worried that Dale might try something on the way to the Center but it seemed his toughness didn't extend to challenging a gun.

In the lot, Larry dialed the sheriff. He spoke into the phone, relaying the information to the dispatcher about Dale's apprehension.

As they waited, a few flies buzzing in the stillness were the only thing convincing Frannie that time was passing. The parking lot was mostly empty, being mid-afternoon on a weekday.

Dale shifted position a couple of times and finally said, "They can't do anything to me. I'm innocent."

"Shut up," Larry said.

Sorenson's car pulled in to the lot, and she got out along with one of her deputies, a big man with the start of a pot belly but the look of being able to hold his own. He snapped the handcuffs on Dale while the sheriff arrested him for suspicion of murder and Mirandized him. Larry handed her Dale's gun while giving her a rundown of his capture.

"We'll see if he has anything more to say as soon as the techs are done with that camera bag."

Dale scoffed and the deputy firmly marched him to the car. The sheriff said she would let them know what developed and Larry and Frannie headed back down the path to the campground. Frannie breathed deeply as she realized how tense she had been. She still questioned Dale's involvement but his behavior was so erratic that she was relieved to be rid of him.

When they reached their site, Mickey, Jane Ann and Nancy were playing dominoes, Donna had headed to her camper for a nap, and Rob and Ben had gone fishing. Frannie and Larry related their latest encounter to a small, but rapt audience and then joined in the game.

After being skunked by Nancy three times in a row, they stacked the pieces in the tin box while discussing supper. They had decided earlier in the day on a taco bar and Mickey already had the meat cooking. Nancy said now that she would put together a bowl of fresh fruit. Larry and Frannie were providing the lettuce and other fixings, Donna was taking care of the tortillas.

Larry and Mickey were in the midst of an argument about which of them made the hottest salsa when Larry's phone rang. He looked at the screen, puzzled, and said, "Hello?"

As he listened, he got up from the picnic table and moved away from the group. When he returned, he said, "Well!"

"What?" Frannie asked. She knew it was news and he was going to try and drag it out.

"That was the sheriff. They've released Dale."

"I'm not too surprised but on what basis?" Frannie said.

"They got the report on the camera bag. Dale's prints aren't on it, and there are no photos of him in either of the cameras in the bag. There are a couple of shots of the trailer but nothing incriminating. Since they found it outside, anyone could have put it there."

Jane Ann said, "How about that meth lab in the log cabin trailer?"

Larry nodded. "There are some shots of that trailer and people coming out that will be good evidence in that case."

"So they could also be the murderers," Mickey said.

Larry shrugged. "She didn't mention whether they found anyone else's prints on it."

"But if the meth dealers had the bag, why leave the incriminating evidence in it?" Frannie said.

"No one said you have to be a mental giant to make meth," Nancy said.

"There's one other thing," Larry said.

"For heaven's sake," Frannie elbowed him in the ribs. "What?"

He held his side in mock pain. "The camera bag was apparently used to knock Virginia into the machinery. They found her blood on it."

Chapter Twenty

They all sat quiet for a minute. "No wonder it disappeared," Frannie said. "It wasn't the photos at all."

"Maybe not," he agreed. "Can't say for sure." They rehashed what they knew but nothing seemed to fit. They planned to go back to Farrell's after supper to see Jonie's 'final' performance, so the tacos needed to be started.

Farrell's Tavern seemed especially busy for a week night. In spite of the dim light, two couples played cards in one corner, and a couple of rough looking men argued the merits of the local stock car drivers at the bar. Two women shared fries and burgers with three kids. One of the kids tried to stick a french fry in his sister's ear while the mothers exchanged important gossip, oblivious of the kids. The scent of beer and fried food suffused the air.

Mary Louise and Jim had joined the group and they found a large table near the back wall. Jonie was into her first set when they came in and she gave them a little wave from the stage. After all, this wasn't Carnegie Hall. Ben and Mickey went to the bar for pitchers of beer and soda, while Jane Ann scooped up free baskets of popcorn from an antique-looking popper in the corner.

As Frannie's eyes adjusted to the light, she noticed Dale and his dad at a table off to the side. Dale stared into a glass of ice water while Mel, chin in hand, gazed up at Jonie with a look that reminded Frannie of the old Mickey Rooney movies.

Mickey, serious for once, said, "You know, I think she's got a pretty good voice, if she wasn't trying so hard to do her impression of country."

Mary Louise agreed, and Jim said, "She had a wonderful voice in high school and people always thought she would go places. If you had heard her then, it's almost painful to listen to her now." He pulled out his pipe. "Matter of fact, I think I'll go out for a smoke." And he hefted his bulk out of the little chrome chair.

Jonie introduced her next song. "Sum of ya know Ah'm planning ta leave Minnesota next week and take my career to Nashvul. Ah'll miss y'all and Ah want to dedicate this next song to a special friend, Mel Dubrak. Heah's my version of 'Ah'll be Seeing Y'all.'" As the recorded background music picked up, Mel sat up straight looking surprised and confused. Frannie felt sorry for him.

Jonie launched into the song, and Frannie realized that the title Jonie had mangled with her fake drawl was the World War II era song, "I'll be Seeing You." All semblance of the drawl gone, Jonie transformed into a Forties torch singer. Her voice, husky and low at the beginning, soared in spots with a quality that Frannie had not heard in her previous numbers. She really *could* sing. Conversations and laughter in the crowd subsided, all eyes on the stage, except for Mel who fidgeted and looked down. When Jonie finished, he glanced at her, dropped his eyes again quickly, and said something to his son.

The silence of the crowd continued for a moment until recorded country music came over the speakers and the whole room exploded in applause. Jonie smiled broadly, gave a little bow, wiped a real tear from her cheek and stepped down from the low stage. She bent over a nearby table, smiling and nodding, accepting good wishes and continued from table to table around the front of the establishment.

Frannie got up to get more popcorn and when she turned around, noticed a familiar figure standing near the front door. Richard Ellis-Reynolds. Dale Dubrak apparently noticed him at the same time, and the fear Frannie and Larry had glimpsed that afternoon returned tenfold to his face. So. Richard was the man who had threatened Dale, the man who 'knows people.'

Dale leaned over to his father and frantically whispered to him, indicating Richard with a jerky bob of his head.

By this time, Jonie had reached Richard and stretched up to give him a kiss on his cheek, her eyes shining. He smiled but his eyes seemed almost menacing. Mel jumped out of his chair and headed across the room to them. Frannie set the popcorn down and pulled her phone out of her pocket. She looked back at her own table on the other side of the room, hoping to catch

Larry's eye but he had his back to the scene, deep in conversation with Mickey.

She dialed 911 and said in a low voice to the dispatcher, "Tell the sheriff this is Frannie Shoemaker and there's trouble brewing out at Farrell's." She punched the phone off and watched the scene unfolding at the door, unsure of what to do.

Mel was much smaller than Richard but had managed to get up into Richard's face. Frannie couldn't hear Mel's words but the tone was threatening. Richard had grabbed Jonie around the waist and had pulled her to his side, his eyes hooded and his expression disdainful as he let Mel rant for a minute. Jonie's expression went from delight to terror as Mel talked and Richard said something low and slow.

Mel raised his hands, palms out, and backed away. It was then that Frannie saw the small knife in Richard's other hand, pointed at Jonie's stomach. She looked back at Larry—too far away—and could not think of any way to intervene that would not endanger Jonie. She knew now the sheriff couldn't arrive in time.

The door crashed open. Richard was knocked slightly off balance. Big Jim Larson filled the doorway and wrapped Richard from behind in a literal bear hug, forcing him to drop the knife. Frannie scrambled for it, dropping her phone and knocking popcorn onto the rough board floor.

By the time the rest of the crowd realized what was happening, it was all over. Jim forced Richard down in a chair and held him there. The disdain and arrogance vanished from Richard's face; only disbelief remained. Mel faced him, his arms around a sobbing Jonie, and harangued him.

"You murderer! You murdered those women and my Jonie was going to be next!"

Richard shook his head. "No, I didn't—"

"Liar!" Mel screamed. "You threatened my boy not to tell! You are nothing but..." he searched for a word vile enough but spat out "*scum!*" in frustration.

Frannie went over to Mel. "Mel, the sheriff will be here soon. It's all over. You and Jonie need to sit down. She needs you right now."

Mel looked at her and his face softened. He nodded and led Jonie back to his table. Larry and the others had reached the front and gathered around Jim, patting him on the back, Mary Louise giving him a hug. The sound of sirens cut the night while the stunned crowd replayed events and speculated in hushed tones.

Sheriff Sorenson put handcuffs on Richard and turned to Frannie.

"I would like you and your husband to follow me to our headquarters and give us a deposition about what happened here tonight." She peered around the dim bar and spotted Mel and Jonie. "Mel," she called, "I need you, Jonie, and Dale to come down and give statements too."

Mel frowned. "Now?"

"Yes, *now*," the sheriff grinned. "Why? Are you that busy?"

Mel smiled back. "Not really." They followed the sheriff out the door.

After separately writing down their recollections of the nights events, Frannie and Larry were taken to an observation room. The deputy explained that the sheriff wanted them to watch Richard's interrogation.

"She thinks you might notice something because you've been watching him."

Larry stood while Frannie took a hard chair in front of the two-way mirror. In the next room, the sheriff sat across a simple wooden table from Richard.

"So, Richard, tell me what happened that morning. How did you happen to murder two women in cold blood?"

"I didn't murder them…both." He looked down at his hands and then up at her, the old arrogance back.

She tilted her head and raised an eyebrow. "Tell me what you did do."

He sighed deeply and looked away.

"I was supposed to meet Val at 9:30. On my way in, I heard Valerie screaming at her sister."

"How did you —?"

"Know it was Valerie? She was yelling about her sister impersonating her and breaking up with me. Valerie told me Friday night that's what happened four years ago. I never even knew she had a twin until that afternoon."

"And then?"

He leaned back and crossed his arms. "I heard a horrible crunch and came around the corner to see...Val on the floor, her head in the machinery, blood all over. Her sister was standing there with that camera bag."

Frannie looked at her husband. "He looks like he's reporting the death of his goldfish."

"How did you know which one was which?" the sheriff asked.

He leaned forward on the table and folded his hands and cocked his head. "The one on the floor was wearing the necklace I gave her."

"Then what?"

"I got out of there—the sister turned around and she was wild! I think she was crazy."

"I don't think so," the sheriff said quietly. She tapped a paper laying on the table in front of her.

Richard straightened up. "What do you mean?"

"I don't think you left. We have another witness," she said.

"He's lying."

"*Who* is lying, Richard?"

"That worthless kid. I left by the tunnel. I knew about it from my grandfather. That kid was hanging out down there—probably doing drugs or something. I told him to keep his mouth shut. I knew how it looked. But I didn't kill Valerie."

Mary Sorenson leaned back in her chair and stared at him, tapping a pencil on the table. "Actually, you did. The woman on the floor was Virginia. The one you strangled before going in the tunnel was Valerie."

Finally a crack in Richard's cool demeanor. "What? I didn't…"

"*Before* you went in the tunnel, you grabbed Valerie's scarf and strangled her with it. The kid heard her beg you —try to tell you who she really was. But you thought she was Virginia, that she had removed a meal ticket from your grasp again."

Realization dawned. Richard looked at her speechless.

"Why did you take the camera bag?"

Richard shrugged, shook his head, looked away.

"Richard?"

"I don't know," he mumbled finally. "I didn't think— I didn't mean to—," he composed himself again. "I want to call my lawyer."

The sheriff nodded to a deputy in the corner of the room to take Richard away. She sat for a moment and then left the room to join the Shoemakers, speaking to another deputy on the way in.

"What do you think?" she asked them.

"I think you have him," Larry said.

Frannie nodded. "It makes sense. It explains the two different MOs."

Larry raised his eyebrows at that and smiled. "She watches a lot of *CSI* and *Law and Order*."

Frannie smirked at that. "Sounds like he grabbed the camera bag without thinking and then had to get rid of it so decided to try and frame Dale."

The sheriff agreed. "It will be up to the court but I'm inclined to believe him. He's a sleaze, but I don't think he premeditated murder. Dale's statement makes it all pretty clear." The sheriff filled them in on a few other details and then said, "Well, thanks for your help. The deputy will take you back to the campground now — Mel and his crew just left."

Chapter Twenty One
Late Tuesday Night

Frannie and Larry pulled into the campsite. Ben and Mickey had built a roaring fire and chairs had been found for the Larsons, Dale, Mel, and Jonie. Mel had repeated his part in the adventure several times, each version more dramatic, while Jonie clung to his arm and gazed at him with adoring eyes.

Mary Louise said, "Well, Jim had a lot to do—"

"Hush, dear," Jim patted her hand. "Mel is the real hero here."

His wife smiled and said, "You're right."

Dale sat nodding while Larry summarized Richard's story.

"So you *were* there...in the tunnel," Frannie said to him.

He shrugged. "I guess."

His father sat forward in his chair. "Son, he could have killed you too!"

"I don't think so," Dale said. "He saw me when he climbed down in the tunnel and he was pretty shook up. He just said I'd better keep my mouth shut or his Chicago mob friends would come after me."

"He was in a hurry to get out of there. He went through the tunnel and back up the hill by the bird watching area to the parking lot where he'd left his truck," Larry said.

"And had plenty of time to get back to the campground before we did," Frannie added.

"Sorenson says there's no evidence he has any connection to Chicago gangsters," Larry assured Dale.

Nancy said, "So he did love Valerie?" glancing at Jonie as she spoke. But the singer seemed oblivious to anyone but Mel.

"No," said Frannie. "I think he is just a fortune-hunting scumbag. Claire, the woman who came with him, is rich but isn't interested in marriage. Valerie and Virginia inherited quite a bit of money from their parents. Jonie told him she is the only heir to her uncle's estate. I think he may be in money trouble back in Chicago so he's just looking for a rich wife. His anger got out of control because he thought Virginia had removed Val from the list of candidates."

Now she had Jonie's attention. "That no-good creep!"

Larry said, "The sheriff told me that the gun was registered to Virginia and only her fingerprints were on it."

"What gun?" Jane Ann asked. The others looked surprised too.

Larry explained about the small gun in the backpack.

Frannie added, "It's possible that Virginia went to the rendezvous planning to kill Richard."

"Oh, my," said Nancy.

"That's one way of putting it," Mickey said.

"But," Donna frowned, "what about the people in the meth lab? They didn't have anything to do with this?"

"Not the murders," Larry said. "They have been picked up in Illinois."

"So they knew or suspected that the twins had photos of them and broke into the trailer in case there was something incriminating them," Ben said.

Larry nodded. "Change of subject. What's our departure plan tomorrow?"

"We have to get going early. Rob has a dentist appointment in the afternoon," Donna said.

"And I have clients to see in the evening," Ben said. "We did some packing up when we got back from Farrell's so we're pretty much ready to go."

Frannie looked around the campsite and realized that a lot of the camping implements had disappeared.

"I don't think it would take us long to get ready," Larry said and turned to Frannie. "Did you want to hang around for a while tomorrow or get going early?"

She smiled. "An early start is fine with me. I think I'm ready for the couch and a few boring days."

"After the laundry's done," Jane Ann reminded her.

Dale turned to Frannie. "I'm very sorry about the attack on you. We just don't like some of the stuff the government does, and y'know, some of the Muslim ideas are good."

"I understand," Frannie said, "but there are other ways to go about change."

"Speaking of change," Jonie said, "Mel has convinced me that country is not my style. I got a pretty good response from the crowd tonight on that last song, so I may try for some gigs around here doing more Thirties and Forties stuff."

"Jonie, that's great," Frannie jumped in. "That was beautiful tonight. Much more your style."

Mel grinned. "That's what I told her. I'm gonna be her manager. Well, we'll say good night—nice meetin' all of you. I think we're ready to turn in," he said and he helped Jonie to her feet in her wobbly heels.

They said goodbye, and as Mel, Jonie, and Dale started down the road. Mickey crooned, "We'll be seeing you...In all the old familiar places..." They could hear Jonie's giggles long after the trio disappeared in the darkness.

HAPPY CAMPER TIPS

Several readers have commented that, while they like the 'Happy Camper Tips,' it is somewhat distracting to have them at the end of each chapter. So, in this book, I have put them all in one place. Less distraction and it should be easier to find one that you want to refer to later.

Happy Camper Tip #1

There's great appeal in the image of the Happy Wanderer when camping: taking off on a whim and stopping wherever it suits you. But for most of us, camping is primarily on the weekends when campgrounds are crowded, and hauling a gas guzzler many miles with no reserved site doesn't leave many options. Cruising around an area looking for sites is cost prohibitive.

Fortunately, most state and national park campgrounds, as well as private establishments now have online reservations systems. Iowa state parks even have photos of every site. The website, Reserve America, has lots of state, federal and private sites, www.reserveamerica.com. Federal campsites can also be reserved at *www.Recreation.gov*.

Different entities have varying reservation windows, from three months to a year so be sure you know what the requirements are. Many sites have information as to the size, shade, and degree of slope that a camper can expect.

A word of caution: most campground maps appear to have been drawn on the back of a napkin from memory. Two sites that look close together or right across the road from each other on the map may in reality be a mile apart. Or on top of each other.

Happy Camper Tip #2

For most of us, firewood is an absolute necessity for camping. In recent years, the emerald ash bore has posed a major threat to our forests, especially in the Midwest. Consequently, many states have posed bans on out-of-state firewood. Some campgrounds don't allow any firewood brought in. Observe this ban. Many parks sell firewood, and there are often private sources in areas around parks.

Happy Camper Tip #3

Camping offers opportunity for wonderful pictures. I keep an 8 x 8 scrapbook of each year's trips, and include photos, journal entries about weather and experiences, and sometimes minitiarized park or campground maps. Brochures from places visited can be stuck between the pages. We enjoy looking back over past trips and they are also useful for settling campfire arguments over who was where, when.

Happy Camper Tip #4

Sometimes inclement weather and sometimes just an itch to explore push many campers out for short road trips. Neighboring towns, even small ones, often boast delightful museums, antique shops, and interesting restaurants. And who could pass up a visit to Rutabaga Days, a bottle cap museum, or the birth place of Jesse James? I didn't make these up. The growth of the wine industry in the Midwest has spawned a corresponding tourist business. Many wineries, often located on scenic Grant Wood-esque hills, supplement their income by hosting musicians in pleasant outdoor gardens or on decks and stage wine and food-tastings. Check the Internet for the local Chamber of Commerce information on what you might be missing if you never leave the campground. A few parks hand out flyers with this information; those who don't are missing the boat—er, camper.

Happy Camper Tip #5

On the level: Getting an RV level can be a challenge but is extremely important for the functioning of the mechanicals: the refrigerator and the water system especially. In addition, it is much more convenient to be able to open cabinets without danger of dire injury, sleep with one's head above one's feet, and lay a pencil on a counter and have it stay there. There are commercial levelers that are nice and convenient, but expensive. We carry a couple of boards that can be used under the wheels on the low side to get close.

Happy Camper Tip #6

Compact, lightweight storage is a constant issue in an RV. We are becoming more and more entangled in a web of charger cords. I made a hanging thingamagig with labeled pockets for each charger — like one of those shoe caddies that hangs over a door, only smaller. It hangs next to an outlet on the end counter and I can tell by glancing at the pockets if we have all the necessary chargers before we leave. It is made of upholstery material and has loops at the top that hook on cup hooks installed under the counter.

Happy Camper Tip #7

Jane Ann's Apple Bars: Combine two cups whole wheat flour, one-fourth cup toasted wheat germ, two teaspoons baking soda, one teaspoon cinnamon, one teaspoon salt, and one-half teaspoon nutmeg. Set aside. In a large bowl, combine four cups diced apples, 1 cup sugar, 1 cup brown sugar, 1/2 cup oil, 1 cup chopped walnuts, 2 eggs and 1 teaspoon vanilla. Add flour mixture and blend well with a wooden spoon. Spread in a greased 13 x 9 pan and bake about 50 minutes at 350.

Travels well in canoes. Also good with butter pecan ice cream on top.

Happy Camper Tip #8

Balsamic marinated salmon filets—Whisk together a couple of tablespoons of brown sugar, three tablespoons of balsamic vinegar, one fourth cup of olive oil, two tablespoons of soy sauce and a tablespoon or so of honey. Pour over washed salmon filets in a plastic bag and marinate in the refrigerator for one to two hours. Grill over medium coals about ten minutes or until done, turning once.

Happy Camper Tip #9

Don't get bugged! One of the greatest annoyances of spending much time outdoors is the insect kind. In the spring and early summer in Iowa, gnats become the state bird and everyone has their own home remedies. My favorite is vanilla. Gnats don't like it and you smell like a cookie. What could be better? Some people say it has to be the real vanilla or the clear type, but I find that the cheap imitation, brown kind works just as well. It also doubles as a fake tan if you put it on evenly. And as a corollary to this tip, those cardboard cut-out evergreens sold as air fresheners for cars in the vanilla scent do a fairly good job just hanging on your lawn chair. Fits in with the woodsy theme, too.

Happy Camper Tip #10

Veggie Pancakes—These are delicious, healthier than regular pancakes, and can be made ahead and warmed up. Grate two cups of zucchini and one cup of carrots. Add one cup of corn—frozen works best. Stir in one egg, two tablespoons of plain yogurt, one half teaspoon of salt and one eighth teaspoon of pepper. Combine one half cup of flour, one half cup of corn meal and two teaspoons of baking powder and add to veggie mixture. Stir well and add one half cup of cheese.

In a skillet with a small amount of oil, use a scant quarter cup of batter for each pancake and flatten slightly with a fork. Cook about three minutes on a side and drain on paper towels. Store in the refrigerator between layers of waxed paper and reheat in the microwave. Excellent with butter and syrup or ranch dressing.

Happy Camper Tip #11

Those of us who have to winterize and store our campers for the non-camping season are faced with a mighty task. Everything that might freeze or be attractive to Friends of the Forest (mice, etc.) must be removed. This includes liquids and foodstuffs, of course, but also most paper items: napkins, paper towels, magazines. But our camping group swears by dryer sheets. We put in one or two in every cupboard and cubbyhole and have never had an invasion from Mickey and his friends. That would NOT be Jane Ann's husband; rather the rodent type.

Happy Camper Tip #12

Step it up: As a result of space and traveling constraints, the folding metal steps that come on many travel trailers and other RVs are narrow and shallow. We like to cook and eat every meal outside possible, but this necessitates a lot of carrying in and out and negotiating those silly steps. We bought our trailer used, and the previous owner had cleverly devised a better step system. He cut boards wider and deeper than each step, notched them to fit around the side supports, and covered them with outdoor carpet. They attach through the holes in the steps with bolts and wing nuts and take about ten minutes to attach during our set-up. Besides making exit and entry less precarious, they provide extra seating—well worth the time and effort.

Happy Camper Tip #13

Useful gadgets: Like every past time, camping has produced a variety of gadgets, some very clever and some more trouble than they're worth. One of my favorites is the folding wagon: a collapsible frame with a canvas bed that is great for hauling firewood from camper or truck to fire ring. It can also be used to haul children and/or groceries and takes up very little space when folded. Another large item that we would not travel without is a metal folding utility table. It normally sits right by the trailer under the outdoor outlet, providing a place for the coffee pot, a crockpot, and cooking in the electric skillet. A mini-blender can be used for breakfast smoothies and quick homemade salad dressings.

Happy Camper Tip #14

Dine in Style: There is nothing wrong with roughing it, but if you like to add a little 'glam' to your meals in the woods without too much effort, there are lots of ways to do that. Want cloth napkins? Bandanas come in multiple colors and wash up well. Saves on the use of paper products as well. Add these to a bright vinyl cloth and you would think you were in a sidewalk cafe in Paris. Sort of. I keep an old, small blue spatterware coffee pot in the camper and often cut flowers, grasses, small branches — whatever is blooming in my yard right before a trip, wrap the stems in wet paper towels and put them in a plastic bag in the refrigerator while traveling. Once we arrive, they reside in the pot and provide a rustic, but bright, spot of color. Finally, what gourmet meal would be complete without candles? There a lots of cute outdoor candles but just a glass jar with a little sand or a few pebbles and a votive will do the trick.

Happy Camper Tip #15

One of the advantages of camping, especially away from urban areas, is the great view of the stars. State and national parks offer wonderful programs on nature themes and sometimes have a stargazing walk. You may also be able to spot the International Space Station going over, a very impressive sight. You can find out where and when to look by entering the zip code of where you will be camping on: http://spotthestation.nasa.gov/sightings/#.UgNj7lNZXC4

Happy Camper Tip #16

Campfire Mac 'n' Cheese: I've tried a couple of different methods, and this one seems the easiest. At home, cook sixteen ounces of macaroni rinse and drain well, and put in a zipper bag. Chill. Oil a cast iron Dutch oven well and layer 1/3 of the macaroni, two or three pats of butter, salt and pepper and about 1/3 cup of shredded cheese. I like a blend like cheddar/jack. Repeat twice.Pour about a cup of milk over the whole thing. Cover and cook over the fire or in the coals until cheese is melted and mixed in with milk. This is fairly conservative on the cheese so you may want more. A big hit with picky kids.

Happy Camper Tip #17

Entertaining the kids: I figure there can't be too many hints on this subject. I saw this one somewhere on the internet. Make a night-time ring toss game by putting glow sticks in empty plastic water or soda bottles. You can then fill them with water to increase the glow and make them less tippy. Make circles out of other glow sticks for the rings. You can also use glow sticks to make the line on the ground to stand behind when trying to ring the bottles.

Scavenger hunts are a favorite time-tested activity and can be used to improve awareness of nature. Include on the list sticks with a certain shape, different rock shapes, varieties of tree leaves, pine cones, and something the finder considers a treasure. You can even require a couple of pieces of man-made litter and help the environment at the same time.

Happy Camper Tip #18

Red and White Oatmeal Bars: Melt two sticks of butter or margarine in a large microwave-safe bowl. Add one cup of white and one cup of brown sugar and stir well. Add two eggs, one teaspoon of vanilla, one-half teaspoon each of baking powder, baking soda, salt, and cinnamon, and one-fourth teaspoon nutmeg and mix. Stir in one cup of white flour, one cup of whole wheat flour, and one and a half cups rolled oats. Add one and a half cups white chocolate chips and one cup dried cranberries. Spread in a greased 9 x 13 pan. Bake at 350 for 35-40 minutes and cut into bars when cool. These store well and are a big hit with adults and kids alike. And like most desserts, they're even better with ice cream or whipped cream.

Happy Camper Tip #19

Recycling containers for camping purposes is environmentally sound and cheap. Some food items can be purchased in containers that can be reused when empty for storage of leftovers. Plastic jars with screw-on lids are especially useful and lightweight. Tic-Tac containers can be used for small amounts of spices. Other low-cost ideas that save space: waxed paper and plastic wrap boxes actually come with punch-in holes on the ends. Mount plastic adhesive hooks sideways with the open ends facing each other to a wall or inside a cabinet and slip the boxes into the hooks. Or store vertically in plastic magazine holders. Collapsible plastic containers take up little room until you pop them open for storing leftovers. Hanging bags with compartments for shoes can be used for tools, cords, or other small items that tend to get lost. You can even mount one over a headboard and use it for glasses, watches, or remotes if you don't have nightstands.

Happy Camper Tip #20

The Burden River and the bike trail are based on the Root River Trail in southeastern Minnesota. There really is an old power plant, a tunnel and an environmental learning center, but farther upriver than depicted here. Deborah does not work at the center and the people there are very helpful. Burdensville is based on the delightful town of Lanesboro, and you can find the pie shop in Whalen.

ACKNOWLEDGMENTS

There is no way I can adequately thank all the people who supported and helped me on this book, but of course I will try. Several people in Lanesboro, Minnesota supplied valuable information; especially the staff at the wonderful Eagle Bluff Environmental Learning Center and the volunteers at the Lancaster Historical Museum for background on the 1915 Root River Power Plant. And I borrowed names from several friends and readers: Valerie Lanning and Virginia Miehe, both diehard walkers but not twins or photographers, graciously consented to be murdered. Mary Larson, Deb McCabe Musser, Joan Rump and Mary Sorenson volunteered (and won the chance!) on my website to be characters in Peete and Repeat.

My husband, Virginia Miehe, and Marcia Stientjes were my early readers and all made important catches and suggestions. The cover art was again the wonderful work of my sister Gretchen and pulled together and formatted by my sister Libby. And I need to mention our camping friends who unwittingly provide much of the material for my books. Finally to my readers for their great and honest reviews and feedback, thank you all.

OTHER BOOKS BY THE AUTHOR
The award-winning Frannie Shoemaker Campground Mysteries:

Bats and Bones: An IndieBRAG Medallion Honoree. Frannie and Larry Shoemaker are retirees who enjoy weekend camping with their friends in state parks in this new cozy mystery series. They anticipate the usual hiking, campfires, good food, and interesting side trips among the bluffs of beautiful Bat Cave State Park for the long Fourth of July weekend — until a dead body turns up. Confined in the campground and surrounded by strangers, Frannie is drawn into the investigation. Frannie's persistence and curiosity helps authorities sort through the possible suspects and motives, but almost ends her new sleuth career — and her life — for good. As a bonus, each chapter ends with a camping tip or recipe — some useful, some not so much.

Peete and Repeat: An IndieBRAG Medallion Honoree. A biking and camping trip to southeastern Minnesota turns into double trouble for Frannie Shoemaker and her friends as she deals with a canoeing mishap and a couple of bodies. Strange happenings in the campground, the nearby nature learning center, and an old power plant complicate the suspect pool and Frannie tries to stay out of it--really--but what can she do? After all, she is only curious, but sometimes it isn't just cats who have trouble with that!

The Lady of the Lake: An IndieBRAG Medallion honoree, 2014 Chanticleer CLUE finalist) A trip down memory lane is fine if you don't stumble on a body. Frannie Shoemaker and her friends camp at Old Dam Trail State Park and take in the county fair. But, Donna becomes the focus of a murder investigation and Frannie wonders if the police shouldn't be looking closer at the victim's many enemies.

To Cache a Killer: Geocaching isn't supposed to be about finding dead bodies. But when retiree, Frannie Shoemaker go camping, standard definitions don't apply. A weekend in a beautiful state park in Iowa buzzes with fund-raising events, a search for Ninja turtles, a bevy of suspects, and lots of great food — and a body.

A Campy Christmas: A Holiday novella. The Shoemakers and Ferraros plan to spend Christmas in Texas and then take a camping trip through the Southwest. But those plans are stopped cold when they are snowbound in a campground in Missouri.

The Space Invader: A cozy/thriller mystery! The starry skies over New Mexico, the "Land of Enchantment," may hold secrets of their own. The Shoemakers and the Ferraros, on an extended camping trip, find themselves picking up a souvenir they don't want and taking sidetrips they didn't plan on.

We are NOT Buying a Camper! A prequel to the Frannie Shoemaker Campground Mysteries. Frannie and Larry

Shoemaker have busy jobs, two teenagers, and plenty of other demands on their time and sanity. Larry's sister and brother-in-law pester them to try camping for relaxation-- time to sit back, enjoy nature, and catch up on naps. After all, what could go wrong? Join Frannie as "RV there yet?" becomes "RV crazy?" and she learns that going back to nature doesn't necessarily mean a simpler life.

Happy Camper Tips and Recipes: All of the tips and recipes from the first four Frannie Shoemaker books in one convenient paperback or Kindle version that you can keep in your camping supplies!

The Time Travel Trailer Series

The Time Travel Trailer: (A Chanticleer 2015 Cygnus award finalist and an IndieBRAG Medallion Honoree) A 1937 vintage camper trailer half hidden in weeds catches Lynne McBriar's eye when she is visiting an elderly friend Ben. But after each remodel, sleeping in the trailer lands Lynne and her daughter Dinah in a previous decade — exciting, yet frightening.

Trailer on the Fly: (An IndieBRAG Medallion Honoree) How many of us have wished at some time or other we could go back in time and change an action or a decision or just take back something that was said? But it is what it is. There is no rewind, reboot, delete key or any other trick to change the past, right?

Lynne McBriar can. She buys a 1937 camper that turned out to be a time portal. When she meets a young woman who suffers from serious depression over the loss of a close friend ten years earlier, she has the power to do something about it. And there is no reason not to use that power. Right?

THANK YOU

For taking your time to share Frannie and Larry's adventures. Just as the sound of a tree falling in the forest depends on hearers, a book only matters if it has readers. Please consider sharing your thoughts with other readers in a review or emailing me at karen.musser.nortman@gmail.com. My website at www.karenmussernortman.com provides updates on my books, my blog, and photos of our for-real camping trips.

Free Download

You can get a free copy of the first
Frannie Shoemaker Campground Mystery,
BATS AND BONES,
if you sign up for my Favorite Readers email list to receive occasional notices about my new books and special offers.

Go to this link:
www.karenmussernortman.com

ABOUT THE AUTHOR

Karen Musser Nortman is the author of the Frannie Shoemaker Campground cozy mystery series, including the BRAGMedallion honoree, *Bats and Bones*. After previous incarnations as a secondary social studies teacher (22 years) and a test developer (18 years), she returned to her childhood dream of writing a novel. The Frannie Shoemaker Campground Mysteries came out of numerous 'round the campfire' discussions, making up answers to questions raised by the peephole glimpses one gets into the lives of fellow campers. Where did those people disappear to for the last two days? What kinds of bones are in this fire pit? Why is that woman wearing heels to the shower house?

Karen and her husband Butch originally tent camped when their children were young and switched to a travel trailer when sleeping on the ground lost its romantic adventure. They take frequent weekend jaunts with friends to parks in Iowa and surrounding states, plus occasional longer trips. Entertainment on these trips has ranged from geocaching and hiking/biking to barbecue contests, balloon fests, and buck skinners' rendezvous. Frannie and Larry will no doubt check out some of these options on their future adventures.

More information is available on her website at www.karenmussernortman.com.